ROMANCES OF THE METAPHYSICALS

BOOK I:

OUTER SPACE
AT THE
END OF TIME

LARRY RINEHART

Introduction and Biographical Sketch of
the Author by Jim Henderson, Ph.D.

Cover Art: Background from Jason Lisle, *The Stargazer's Guide to the Night Sky*, p. 68. Polyhedron from *Fundamentals of Mathematics*, ed. Behnke, Bachmann, Fladt and Kunle, Vol. III, p. 280. Composite by author.

TABLE OF CONTENTS

INTRODUCTION

Landmark works of literature spring from seasoned minds and practiced hands. Great authors of fiction harness human imagination to engage, challenge, and edify thoughtful readers. The best bards enlarge the world we think we know. Their tales arc across wide and fabulous landscapes, raise profound questions of meaning and worth, and culminate in visions of transcendent wonder, if not apocalypse. Larry Rinehart's *Outer Space at the End of Time* and the trilogy it initiates descend from a lofty range of seminal texts: Dante's *The Divine Comedy* (1308-1320), Melville's *Moby-Dick* (1851), and metaphysically serious works of science fiction from the last hundred years, such as David Lindsay's *A Voyage to Arcturus* (1920), C. S. Lewis's *Cosmic Trilogy* (1938-1945), and Michael D. O'Brien's *Children of the Last Days* series. Such is the distinguished literary company Larry keeps. He and I invite you to join it—if you have courage and strength for the journey!

The design of Larry's earth-space fiction exemplifies the characteristics of the "romance." The term "novel" is often misapplied to all manner of modern prose fiction. In fact, many of the most popular forms of contemporary fiction—from Harlequin romances and historical novels to science fiction and fantasy—are best categorized as romances. Like the epic and chivalric tales that inspire it, Larry's fiction implicates human protagonists, superior in degree to most of us in terms of their qualities and abilities, in a quest that requires them to encounter and respond to marvelous manifestations of the sacred.

In 1851 Nathaniel Hawthorne offered what has become the quintessential definition of the modern romance, in contradistinction to the novel. Hawthorne famously stated, in his preface to *The House of the Seven Gables*, that romances aim to reveal "the truth of the human heart" and, in pursuit of that aim, freely depart from the constraints of a novel's realism to "mingle the marvelous" with the actual. Henry James went on to elaborate Hawthorne's view when he argued, in his preface to *The American* (1877), that the romance deals with "experience liberated...from the conditions that...drag upon it." As Gillian Beer asserted in *The Romance* (1970), a book as wise as it is slender, the chief concern of romance is to make apparent "the hidden dreams" of the known world, and in doing so, not only to "imitate daily life" but also "to transcend it." The plot and theme of Larry's romance inscribe a marvelous arc that leads from the everyday to the transcendent, and back again.

Northrop Frye, a prolific scholar of the romance, suggested that romances and novels are best distinguished by their different approaches to characterization. In the Fourth Essay of his classic *Anatomy of Criticism* (1957) Frye affirms that "The romancer does not attempt to create 'real people' so much as stylized figures which expand into... archetypes." Larry's four young-adult protagonists in *Outer Space at the End of Time* qualify as romantic heroes and heroines not simply because they pair up and fall in love as the plot unfolds, but more especially because they are larger than life—brighter, braver, and more faithful to their beliefs than humans are generally able to be. Their tale is a classic romantic quest; it turns on surmounting formidable obstacles that stand between the characters and the Holy Grail they seek. The protagonists, with help from wise mentors, prove themselves worthy as the romance powers forward in space and time. Its culminating vision is ultimately revealed, as a timeless moment, in wondrous, sumptuous, precise detail.

Larry Rinehart's rich imagination, his command of the scientific and metaphysical materials from which his tale is fashioned, and his practiced use of romantic devices and narrative style energize Outer Space at the End of Time. The book is a delight to read. In proposing a worthy adventure, and promising (and delivering) a revelation of the highest order, this charming yet challenging Christian romance invites faithful and discerning readers—and demands a sequel. If it please God, may both be manifest in days and years to come!

Jim Henderson, Ph.D.
Durham, North Carolina
New Year's Day, 2020

AUTHOR'S PREFACE

The metaphysical romance upon which the worthy reader is about to embark is above all Christian in conception, and secondarily epic. It is Christian not just because its characters identify as such, but also because it breathes an atmosphere of traditional liturgy and of Christian metaphysical doctrines, while telling the story of an interstellar voyage that includes catechetical instruction by angels, and a Dantesque examination on faith. After which things get really interesting. But the book is also Christian in its portrayal of faithful intellectuals striving toward a synthesis of theology, metaphysics, and the biblical creation sciences of nature, as a foundation for a Christian civilization capable of taking back the intellectual territory that has been ceded by the Church to secular atheism since Galileo and Copernicus. Even the epoch in which our tale is set, and the interpretation of that epoch which renders it epic, are taken from Christian tradition on the End of Time, especially the Russian Orthodox strain. Overall, an important concern in composing *Outer Space at the End of Time* was to incorporate a sampling of the rich intellectual heritage comprised in Christian tradition, with an earnest hope that the worthy reader will find this material enjoyable, edifying, and even inspiring.

According to our epic interpretation the Communist subjugation of Orthodox Russia in 1917, and the sudden collapse of the Soviet regime in 1987 (exactly seventy years later), signaled the near approach of the End (Engleman, *Ultimate Things*). The epic *mythos* of our romance, building upon the Orthodox analysis, extrapolates another seventy years into the future from 1987 in imagining the actual year in which time grinds to a halt with the coming of Christ. This fictive hypothesis is not intended to be prophetic. Another epic feature of the book before us is also not intended prophetically, albeit with a lively hope; and though it plays but a minor role in the narrative it is essential to the aforesaid *mythos* and therefore needs to be addressed. The feature in question is the part played by two specific nations, and by two specific Presidents of those nations, in stabilizing a geopolitical order under which a restoration of spiritual traditions, especially the Christian, is able to flourish briefly—"a flowering before the end." As of this writing it is still unclear whether the two historical Presidents in question are actually working together toward such a goal.

In any case our epic *mythos*, whether or not it proves in any part prophetic, is to be developed further in a sequel, *The Final Fortnight of Years*, which will conclude with the End of Time. A third and final romance, then, could only be some sort of *Paradiso* (*Metaphysicals in Paradise*), though the very thought of undertaking such a commission evokes a certain fear and trembling in your humble author. Nevertheless that, if God sustain the undertaking, is the plan of a trilogy entitled *Romances of the Metaphysicals*, of which the worthy reader has the first Book in hand.

It is needless to say anything about the genre of romance, which has already been admirably covered in the Introduction by my old friend Jim Henderson, whose masterful ability to play two saxophones at once is actually mirrored in the narrative at hand, in a way that solves a perplexing astronomical problem. (Let the reader be on the lookout!). In addition to numerous helpful editorial suggestions, Jim has also supplied a Biographical Sketch of yours truly, which I am somewhat startled to admit is fairly true to character, even if chronicled with a friendly and generous take on the subject. Unlike Oliver Cromwell, I did not insist he put in "warts and all," and I thank him for a noble portrait. Thanks also to my dear wife Donna, a retired teacher, talented watercolorist, and gifted home economist, whose daily companionship is a sturdy support and a bright beam of affection; and who has read the ensuing romance from start to finish, insuring me of its readability while intimating that perhaps a few parts, here and there, could bear skipping over. Behold, another challenge for the worthy reader: which parts would those be? Godspeed!

Larry Rinehart
Dover, Pennsylvania
Ash Wednesday, 2020

PROLOGUE:
THE GRADUATION SPEECH

"Luther-Aquinas Evangelical College, of which you are the tenth graduating class, stands as a shining example of the Christian Restoration in these States, which flowered so surprisingly a decade or more before the founding if this illustrious College. Allow me to recall for you, who are children of this Restoration, a little of the history that has brought you here."

The distinguished greybeard, chosen by the College to address this anniversary class, stood at a podium facing the tiered, semicircular seating in the outdoor chapel, constructed of stone like a primitive amphitheater. The first several tiers in the central section of this construction were occupied by the new graduates, and the balance of the seating by parents and other guests, while the faculty sat in the choir behind the speaker. The mild sunshine of a late May afternoon played over the assembly, as the shadows of tall oaks and hemlocks, just to the west, crept imperceptibly closer. But the greybeard had gained the crowd's attention.

"By the end of the twentieth century, the academic dominance of secular rationalism had not only placed Christians on the defensive in the face of new social norms, but had undercut the Church intellectually by misuse of secular methods in the analysis of divine revelation."

Maxim Lossky-Mendez sat with his fellow graduates, nodding as did many of them in agreement with this point, which he as a religion and theology major was especially well equipped to appreciate. Indeed he was confirmed in his own vocation, not only to seek ordination as an Orthodox priest but to work intellectually for the defense of the full traditional Christian faith, against all attempts to undermine or revise it.

"Scientifically, the dominance of evolutionist theories of the origin of the universe and of terrestrial life was virtually absolute, even though massively documented discrepancies had been widely published. It was impossible to even challenge the Darwinian paradigm in the public schools."

Now it was Christopher Eckhart, seated alphabetically at a slight remove from his friend Maxim, who was uniquely equipped to fathom the scope and severity of the discrepancies to which the speaker alluded in passing. As a philosophy major specializing in the philosophy of science, he approached the natural sciences from the perspective of traditional metaphysics, and he had some thoughts bordering especially on physics, which he intended to pursue.

"Well into the second decade of our own century it appeared to those with an eye for prophecy that the system of the Antichrist, complete with a global tyranny, was falling all too rapidly into place. And yet by the 'twenties, largely facilitated by the concord of two men, two Presidents, a Russian and an American, both Christians and both devoted to the protection of Christians and other minorities—a Restoration of traditional Christianity was underway more or less worldwide."

Sophia Lossky-Mendez sat beside her twin brother Maxim, smiling at the mention of the partnership between Russian and American Christians as the mainspring of the Restoration of traditional faith. With dual majors in astronomy and linguistics, she was somewhat less focused on theology and the Church than was her brother, but she was deeply committed to the Orthodox faith, and her studies would be a contribution to the Christian civilization in its final flowering.

"Of course not everyone claiming to be Christian was pleased by this Restoration, let alone the atheists, and indeed whole nations whose historical roots had been Christian remained unaffected, except in small robust minorities of the faithful. The political trend toward flexible, lightweight federal oversight of neomedieval city-states and regions, allowed for local municipalities to include Biblical teaching in public school, or not, allowing communities to form according to cultural similarity. This has included even Islamic sharia law and, on the other extreme, Nevada."

Seated beside her twin brother Chris, Maria Eckhart was prepared not so much by her mathematics major as by her minor in history, to gauge the significance of the cultural and political developments summarized so succinctly by the speaker. Having grown up in rural Pennsylvania, indeed just an hour's drive from the College, Maria had been blessed personally to live in a mostly-Christian municipality which was friendly, but not accommodating, to non-Christians. For example, traditional Muslims willing to live by municipal law were welcome, but they were not exempt from gentle evangelization.

"In the meantime, established science was forced to concede that it had a terrible problem accounting for the observed degree of order, both in the universe at large and in living organisms, while creation science, much to the contrary, having realized at last its need for metaphysical premises, came into full flower."

Chris Eckhart momentarily turned his gaze from the face of the sagacious orator, to the towering trees westward, the shadows of which still advanced toward the assembly with the sun's declination. That flowering of creation science, he mused, that rigorous reconsideration of the natural order in supernatural light, of physical order in metaphysical light—was precisely the spiritual movement that had captured his intellect and formed his earthly vocation.

"Finally, on the theological front, I must mention two developments that touch directly upon the foundation of this College: First, the recognition by many Evangelicals of the centrality of Martin Luther in the sixteenth-century Reformation, and a significant turning to his sacramental theology in particular, and his mystical understanding of faith. And second, the recognition also by Evangelicals, of the importance of Thomas Aquinas as the premier Christian philosopher of premodernity, whose value has perhaps even increased in view of the turn to metaphysical foundations for the natural sciences in the biblical paradigm, along with the recognition of Luther's philosophical deficiencies as a theologian."

Chris and Maxim caught each other's glance, exchanging enigmatic smiles. The theological developments just epitomized meant very different things to the two friends, since Chris was an orthodox Lutheran evangelical Catholic (his own description), and moreover had adopted St. Thomas Aquinas as his philosophical mentor; while Max maintained certain Eastern reservations about certain philosophical developments in Western theology, preferring his name-saint Maximus Confessor to Chris' Aquinas. Yet the unique spiritual energies of the Restoration had brought together traditional Christians of several kinds, and here he was, graduating from Luther-Aquinas Evangelical!

"The long and the short of all this is that by about 2030 a number of new Christian colleges were being formed and producing graduates, among them your own distinguished College, and these graduates in turn have sustained the Restoration for a remarkable decade. I say this decade has been remarkable, not only for the reestablishment of Christian values in a significant cross-section of regional municipalities, while allowing for different cultural developments in other regions. For what is equally remarkable is the mere duration, however modest, of this Eliatic Restoration in the very face of the gathering menace of the Adversary's system, and the obvious imminence of the End of Time."

Maria drew a long, slow breath, like a slow-motion gasp, as she marveled anew at the historical improbability of the virtually miraculous developments painted by the greybeard's broad brush. Then again, she felt the immense privilege and the corresponding responsibility of living, as a Christian, in such times. Her friend Sophie was thinking about the word "Eliatic", and the analogy underlying the orator's use of it: as Scripture says Elias (or Elijah) will appear before the Day of the Lord, so this Restoration, heralding the End, is called "Eliatic". She also reflected with a smile, that it was the Russian miracle that started it all—the reemergence of Christian Russia from the rubble of the godless Soviet system.

"You who graduate today from Luther-Aquinas Evangelical College bear a sacred obligation to carry forward this flowering of Christian culture in whatever ways the Creator is calling you. We simply do not know how much longer this blessed interval will last, before the final darkness consolidates its power in preparation for our Lord's return. Therefore go forth and work, for the night is coming, and may God bless and protect you all."

The shadows of the westward hemlocks and oaks were just bringing to an end the play of sunlight over the assembled crowd, which after standing to applaud the grand and solemn remarks just concluded, fell silent as the College's chaplain stepped forward to pronounce the Aaronic benediction:

"May the Lord bless you and keep you.
May the Lord make His face to shine upon you
and be gracious unto you.
May the Lord lift up His countenance upon you,
and give you peace,
in the Name of the Father and of the Son
and of the Holy Ghost. Amen."

The jubilation of the new graduates and of their families and friends may have been slightly attenuated by the solemnity of their historical moment as just described; nevertheless, the indomitable energy of youth carried the day. As the assembly dispersed amid mutual congratulations all around, our four protagonists made plans with their parents for an early supper, and advised any interested classmates that the "Metaphysicals" would be at their usual table at the Ox & Swan by eight o'clock that evening for a "valedictory symposium". To clarify this latter advisement, "the Metaphysicals" was the moniker by which this fabulous foursome, this double dynamic duo, had come to be known around the College; and the Ox & Swan was the on-campus tavern named for Thomas Aquinas and Martin Luther, respectively, with reference to Thomas' nickname

"Dumb Ox" and to Luther's fulfillment of the prophecy of Jan Hus that 'a swan will sing'. As for the valedictory symposium, we shall soon have taste of that. Meanwhile, our "Metaphysicals" are off to dine with their families.

CHAPTER ONE:
THE VALEDICTORY
SYMPOSIUM

"One, two, three; but where, my dear Christopher, is the fourth of those who earlier promised to be present at this symposium?" Thus the Reverend Doctor Thomas Killgower, Dean of the College, to Christopher Eckhart, who was seated at table in the Ox & Swan Tavern with the Lossky-Mendez twins. "Our blonde seems to be running a bit late," replied her brother with a smile. "But look: here she is now." Maria's smiling face, ringed with blond curls, peered at her seated friends from behind the broad frame of Dean Killgower, who graciously stepped aside to greet her.

"Am I late?" she asked rhetorically, her bright blue eyes feigning surprise. "For a very important date!" quipped Maxim in reply, as a twinkle of a glance passed between them. But the Reverend Doctor, friend and mentor of the four, was intent upon proceeding with the promised colloquium. Pitchers of beer were brought to table, several dozen interested parties assembled at surrounding tables, and the Dean introduced the proceedings.

The main hall of the Ox & Swan Tavern was roughly thirty feet wide, and extended lengthwise forty-five feet from the bar at one end to the wall opposite, where our Metaphysicals were gathered for the event. The floor and the bar were of local black walnut, as was the wainscoting which rose to table height along the walls, joining the native sandstone which formed the interior face of the structural walls. The ceiling by contrast, was entirely white with large ceiling lights, so that more than adequate illumination was afforded to those seated at the ten or twelve tables, also of walnut, that were arranged upon and amidst the dark woodwork. Centered on the wall behind the bar, and also on the wall opposite, above the table where our Metaphysicals had deployed themselves, hung mirror-image paintings of the same figurative motif, designed to illustrate the peculiar name of the Tavern.

The paintings were large, say five feet wide by two-and-a-half high, and were divided into left and right halves by the image of an open Bible painted in gold at their top centers. In one half of the paintings appeared a great Ox, black and white in analogy to the Dominican habit, recumbent in the manner of "Ferdinand the Bull", but surrounded by books instead of flowers, and instead of sniffing a flower, gazing ardently at the open Bible. The other half portrayed a stout Swan entirely black (except for a piercing blue eye) after the Augustinian habit (and with a Doctor's cap), rampant (in the heraldic sense) with the upper wing touching the Bible, and the lower wing clutching a foaming glass of beer. Standing near the painting on the far side of the hall, Dean

Killgower was seen to clutch a similar glass himself as he introduced the evening's festivity.

After greeting all assembled on behalf of the College, and alluding briefly to the intellectual distinction of the four brand-new graduates who were the occasion of the gathering, the Dean explained that these Metaphysicals would each offer a sampling of what first fruits their studies had born, and perhaps an inkling of where the Lord might thenceforth be leading them. "May the words of their mouths," he concluded, "and the meditations of our hearts, be true and acceptable in Thy sight, O Lord, our Rock and our Redeemer. Amen." Then mentioning that he had asked Maxim to speak first, he raised his glass ceremoniously and took his seat.

Maxim Lossky-Mendez arose from his seat, all six-foot-two of him, broad-shouldered but wiry with curly black hair and quiet brown eyes, and in a voice not so much quiet as reserved, clearly audible yet unassuming, he began by thanking the Dean for the helpful guidance extended to him and to his sister, as Russian Orthodox students in an evangelical-catholic College. He also thanked elder Lavrenty, the Orthodox hermit whose term of residency at the College was the major reason Maxim had been drawn there, for sagacious advice and counsel regarding his own developing vocation. Lavrenty was not then present, but his appearance was expected before the evening was over. Maxim went on to say that he had learned a great deal of theology at Luther-Aquinas, not least with regard to the two theologians for whom it was named—though always with an eye to significant differences from the Orthodoxy of the East. On one hand, he found Luther and the orthodox Lutherans to be closer to the East in some ways than Aquinas was, like believing that the body and blood of Christ are really present in the eucharistic bread and wine, without imposing a philosophical theory of "transubstantiation" upon faith in the words of Christ. And like believing that Christ is really present in the human spiritual heart by faith, which participates in the spiritual presence of Christ—an understanding both Biblical and at least analogous to Eastern teachings on *theosis*, or divinization of the human being by the Holy Spirit. On the other hand, Maxim was compelled to observe that Luther's mystical stress on faith alone had fostered weak doctrines of Church order and of sanctification (the disciplined development of the fruits of the Spirit); and that Luther's contempt for metaphysical speculation in support of faith had facilitated the intellectual surrender of the Reformation churches to the modern secular academy and its axiomatically atheistic sciences. At this point in his discourse, of which the preceding is merely a summary, Maxim noted that his friend Chris might have a word to say on these points, and nodding genially, yielded the floor.

Nearly six inches shorter than his friend, stocky and muscular with longish sand-colored hair, Chris Eckhart rose slowly and paused for a moment before speaking, his deep blue eyes fixed on the table before him. Then drawing a deep breath, he began by admitting that he was no theology major like Max, but he wished to remind his friend that Luther's theological formation had transpired in reaction to the over-emphasis on the accumulation of merit then dominant in the Western church, and that his evangelical mysticism countered this by emphasizing the spiritual annihilation of the believer ("*not I* but Christ", in St. Paul's phrase) and the assignment of all merit to Christ. Now if one is spiritually becoming nothing rather than accumulating merit, the young philosopher argued, one may be somewhat less fixated on residual sin "in the members" and the disciplined development of its eradication, at least to the degree that sanctification is understood in some traditions. Christopher added that he thought ecclesiology was another area of overlap between Lutheran and Eastern traditions, since the Augsburg Confession located the reality of the Church in the assembly of believers around the Word and the Sacraments, and Orthodoxy held that the fullness of the Church is present in every local assembly where the Body of Christ is eucharistically formed.

Maxim, seated to the side of his friend, nodded his agreement with a broad smile, so Christopher went on. To the former's other point, he fully agreed that Luther's contempt for speculative reason, even when subordinated by faith to the authority of Scripture, had lent unfortunate impetus to the secularization of reason in the modernizing West. This was the very reason, he continued, that while he followed Luther theologically on key points, philosophically he was more or less a Lutheran Thomist, without losing sight of certain non-Aristotelian perspectives, including Luther's own neo-Augustinian modes of *esse* or being: namely nature, grace and glory. Chris's own vocation was to the metaphysical analysis of the sciences of nature in the modern sense of "science", especially physics and biology, and he hoped to participate in the "grand unification" of Biblical creation science before the End of Time. He also had some technical speculations he would like to mention, but observed that his friend might wish to reply to his remarks thus far, before he continued. Whereupon he returned to his seat and his glass of beer.

Maxim again towered over the group, still smiling through his dark curly beard, and in a voice both ample and somewhat retiring, he happily admitted that Augustine and Aquinas both knew human knowledge to require participation in the uncreated knowledge of God, in order to be true, although Thomas in Aristotelian fashion limited our knowledge to abstraction from sensory data, while Augustine's notion of knowledge included direct mental intuition of purely intelligible realities, being more Platonic in perspective. Yet neither view, Max argued, was equivalent to the Eastern understanding of *nous* or spiritual intellect, which included direct intuition of the divine, metaphysical, uncreated order, this being in fact an aspect of the aforementioned *theosis*. He did not wish to be overly polemical on the point, but in the spirit of truth he wished to commend this consideration to his learned friend, to whom he yielded the floor. With a quick inclination in Chris' direction, he sat down.

Thanking Maxim for his brotherly counsel, Chris rose to argue, after a thoughtful pause, that it was far from certain that the highest intellection known to the Western metaphysical sages was confined to knowledge of sensory data, created ideas or intelligible realities. Here our philosopher retrieved his beer glass from the table, raised it high in the air, and proposed a toast to his own illustrious namesake, the Meister, whose doctrine of divine knowledge, as he went on to explain after taking one swallow and returning his glass to the table, was precisely what rendered debatable the point advanced by Max. Ambiguous indications in the thought of Augustine and of Aquinas are made explicit in the Meister in his teaching about the transposition or inversion of the created intellect into its uncreated Principle, the Intellect in God, not by human action but by pure uncreated grace. The question remained open, he wished to suggest, whether Meister Eckhart's metaphysical "transposition" did not symbolize the same cognitive reality as the "intuition" of the uncreated order by the spiritual *nous* of the East.

Maxim nodded affably, so Chris proceeded with his final remarks, beginning with the assertion that physics presupposes metaphysics because the actions and processes studied by physics are created realities deriving from uncreated precursors in divine Intellect. Moreover, God's knowing a reality as created was tantamount to his creating it, so the act of creation could be considered an ontology of divine knowledge, that is, an actualization of uncreated possibilities in created processes by God's knowing them as such. Thinking along these lines, our intrepid philosopher continued, it had occurred to him that certain physical processes, such as continuous transportation through spacetime, might have uncreated transpositions which could, if activated, cause something at one place in spacetime to immediately be at another place in spacetime, however distant, without traversing the intervening spacetime, and without duration of time or expenditure of physical energy. These were the technical speculations he had mentioned earlier, and which he intended to pursue further in the quiet of his family farm, along with the rustic pursuits that went with running the latter.

And speaking of his immediate plans, he asked if Max would like to say a few words about his, before the two of them surrendered the floor to the ladies, both of whom he commended warmly for listening with such exemplary patience while the men shared bits of their thinking with the circle of listeners. At this, Maria and Sophia both raised their glasses in acquiescence, and Maxim stood briefly to round out his discourse for the evening. Having earlier offered a few remarks on the titular patrons of the College, and on the Eastern notion of spiritual intellection, the budding theologian wished to mention his name-saint, Maximus Confessor, whose theory of uncreated *logoi* in the eternal *Logos* corresponding to all creatures closely resembled the Western approaches favored by his friend, yet whose overall perspective Max himself was drawn to. He planned to pursue further study of the theology and metaphysics of St. Maximus at an Orthodox seminary back home in

Texas, in order to prepare himself for the priesthood, and for the intellectual defense of the ancient faith and the philosophical forms in which it was formulated. With a friendly glance to all quarters, he raised his glass to the painting on the wall behind, and took his seat.

The Reverend Doctor Killgower now took the opportunity to resume the role of unofficial master of ceremonies for the evening, and with a colorful tartan jacket lending accent to his presence, he explained his logic as to the order in which the four scholars had been asked to speak, namely in the intellectual order of their disciplines. Thus Theology first, then Metaphysics, Mathematics and Astronomy plus Linguistics, with a concluding historical note by the mathematician. Therefore the genders were entirely accidental, and the patience of the ladies was indeed appreciated. With that, he nodded amiably toward Maria and sat down.

Just over five feet tall, with the lithe sturdiness of a gymnast and equestrienne, Maria Eckhart rose from her chair with a slight toss of her blond curls, then stood as if absent-mindedly for a moment, her bright blue eyes twinkling with thought. According to Luther, she began, it is undeniable that the mathematical disciplines are divinely revealed, and for her part she could readily believe it. For by mathematics the human intellect, created in the image of the divine, has concrete knowledge of intelligible forms that sometimes describe nature as known to our senses. Mathematical forms of this kind, Maria continued, demonstrate that God used these ideas (or the uncreated precursors of the ideas we conceive theoretically) in creating the corresponding modes or domains of nature as we know it. If this was not quite clear, no worries were in order, for she intended to furnish a couple of examples.

After another pause with blue eyes atwinkle, she spoke of the Spencer-Brownian calculus of forms, which she described as beginning with a single primordial form whose image is used as a mark in a formal arithmetic, on which is defined a formal algebra, into which the introduction of imaginary values produces self-reentrant algebraic structures, capable of emitting mathematical waveforms implying both time and topology. Maria paused to take a sip from her glass of Augustiner Brau while her audience pondered the remarkable calculus she had just sketched, generating from a single form a whole hierarchy of mathematical structures with obvious analogies to physical processes. Her second example was couched in more conventional terminology, beginning with the notion of set, as an aggregation of elements each of which is also a set, and then relations between sets, from which algebras and topologies can be constructed, as well as geometries not limited to three dimensions, which allows the geometrization of time and the definition of curvature in 4-space, theoretically generating time, matter, and gravity. All of this, she added, got even more exciting in geocentric (earth-centered) coordinates, but she did not wish to steel the thunder of her friend Sophia the astronomer, who was prepared to go into more detail on that very topic. And with an elegant curtsy she resumed her place at the table.

Sophia Lossky-Mendez, like her friend Maria, was a beautiful young woman to behold—each with her own almost archetypal style of feminine beauty. Sophie's hair was dark and curly like her brother's, and she stood a half-foot taller than her petite friend, and slightly bigger-boned, as she directed her big brown eyes from face to face of those assembled, including the Dean and her fellow Metaphysicals, locking them briefly with Chris's deep blues. Then, in alto tones, she began by thanking her mathematical friend for setting the intellectual scene so well for the geocentric white-hole (GWH) cosmology, defined in the framework of general relativity, by which creation cosmologists had developed a class of models explaining how ancient (and distant) stars do not contradict a young earth. Briefly, she said, if God's stretching out of the firmament is interpreted as the expansion of spacetime itself in conjunction with matter ejected from a geocentric white hole, then geometrical effects on the rate of time itself produce the passage of billions of years in distant space while only six days pass on Earth! Sophie paused for effect, then added that if one assumed matter was first created as pure water (H_2O) and with all the molecules magnetically polarized in one direction, then partially collapsed toward the black-hole state before exploding as a white hole, accurate predictions of the magnetic fields of astronomical bodies are obtainable. Again she waited for her words to sink in before proceeding.

It was theories like these that were a Godsend to creation astronomers, our brilliant brunette continued, but astronomers also gaze into outer space. What is the evidence that Earth is the center of the universe? First she noted that deep-space gamma-ray bursts (GRBs) are nearly always in a direct line to a galaxy, as seen from Earth. Second, deep-space surveys have revealed numerous clusters of galaxies arranged in elongated linear structures all pointing toward earth: even secular astronomers call them the "fingers of God", Sophie added with a smile. Her third example of evidence for the geocentricity of the universe was the strong correlation between the structure of the cosmic microwave background (CMB) and the orbit of the Earth. The entire sphere of the geocentric sky, she explained, had a slightly warmer hemisphere and a slightly cooler hemisphere as measured by micro-temperatures of the CMB, and the plane dividing the two hemispheres of the sky is perpendicular to the plane of the earth's orbit! And not only that, she went on, her alto voice rising with excitement, but this basic CMB dipole perpendicular to the Earth's orbit has quadrupole and octupole structures defining another plane perpendicular to the orbital plane, and passing through the two solstice points on the orbit. Since the CMB was considered to originate in the most distant reaches of space-time, this clearly implied the correlation of cosmological structure with a central Earth, as did the other two examples.

Sophia stopped to take refreshment from the glass before her on the table, then looked around the audience again, taking time to answer a few points of clarification regarding the glimpse of creation astronomy she had just offered up.

She apologized for going on at such length, and begged the patience of her auditors for a few further remarks arising from her second major, linguistics, as related to the science of the stars. But in order to do that she required a quick excursion through metaphysics, in which she was no expert but had enjoyed the expert guidance of her philosophical friend Christopher— and here her big brown eyes again locked briefly with his deep blues. The Angelic Doctor Aquinas, she explained, posited that every star was united with an angel, but not as our intellectual soul is united with our body—in other words, the star is not the body of the angel, for angels are bodiless, but the star is subject to being *moved* by the angel. This could refer to locomotion in spacetime, and/or it could refer to internal motions and changes in the intra-stellar processes, which in turn cause modulations in the emitted starlight, across the entire electromagnetic spectrum. Since angels are highly intelligent beings, Sophie reasoned, they were certainly capable of "moving" the stars in which they were stationed, to emit linguistically meaningful signals, perhaps even by complex correlations between changes in signal intensity across the spectrum. It was this kind of "extra-terrestrial intelligence" that our astronomer was interested in looking for, and she was pleased to announce that her mathematical friend Maria would be joining her for graduate study at a distinguished Christian university in the Rocky Mountains, where they would work together in the search for such angelic communications. Then with a deep breath, and a nod toward Maria, she yielded the floor.

As she rose to speak, Maria Eckhart exuded the poise of a gymnast facing a springboard, as again her bright blue eyes sparkled with thought, if perhaps more solemnly this time. She said that Dean Killgower (to whom she nodded deferentially) had asked her to say a few words from the perspective of her minor in history, especially regarding the past century or so. Wrinkles appeared on her forehead through a veil of blond curls, as she began by noting that the history of the past century (roughly 1940-2040) only made sense in the context of several preceding centuries, as when Descartes grounded the certainty of existence in the experience of thinking instead of divine revelation, and then Kant decreed that we can have no knowledge of reality in itself, including God, paving the way for Hegel to reduce reality to a historical dialectic with forward progress, which is the same general notion from which Darwin fabricated a theory of biological evolution, and Marx an ideology of political revolution. If there was indeed a progression in all this, Maria continued, it was the steady ascendancy of a secular reason that more and more explicitly expressed the atheistic premises implicit in its origins, as Luther had warned.

Maria took another sip from her glass of Augustiner, then replaced it on the table. The twentieth century, she said, was best understood in the Russian perspective, of which her knowledge owed much to her theological friend Maxim, whose eyes just then met hers with a reflected twinkle. The overthrow of Russia by an international Communist conspiracy in 1917, ending the line of Christian monarchs extending from Constantine, and involving the murder of millions of Christians, was by traditional interpretation of Biblical prophecies taken as the sign that the End of Time drew near. Yet seventy years later, our ebullient blonde went on, the collapse of the Soviet system found the ancient Orthodox faith alive in the hearts of the Russian people, like an ember under the ashes. A President named Vladimir and the Patriarchs of Moscow oversaw the consolidation of the new Russian republic, a Christian nation tolerating other faiths and ready for peaceful trade— but also ready to defend militarily both itself and other nations unjustly attacked. Then a President named Donald was elected in the States, and Americans learned that an international conspiracy like the one that overthrew Russia had nearly gained control of the United States, having infiltrated all branches of government, intelligence agencies, and communications media. But after the key election, the traitors were brought before military tribunals in possession of irrefutable evidence of their treason, and justice having been served, and the banking system thoroughly reformed, the powers that had successfully kept Russia and America from amicable relations were effectively neutralized. The rest, she laughed, was history. Bowing gracefully all around, she alighted on her chair.

At this point the tartan-clad Reverend Doctor regained the floor, the red, green, navy and yellow of clan Killgower's plaid showing brilliantly under the ceiling lights before the symbolic painting, the rest of the lights in the hall being dimmed for the occasion. Observing that over an hour and a half had been filled by the preceding discourses, the Dean declared a ten-minute recess for the accommodation of various natural necessities, as well as for the Metaphysicals to circulate among their faithful audience, gleaning a couple or three topics of interest for further discussion to round out the evening. As the lights in the hall were brightened to full illumination for the intermission, it appeared that Elder Lavrenty had entered the hall unnoticed, and was seated at a small table in the corner created by one wall of a short entrance corridor, with a half-pint of imperial stout in front of him. Now that the assembly had noticed him, the Elder rose to greet them, raising one hand in a gesture of blessing while reciting the dominical greeting, "Peace be with you." His tall sturdy form was draped in a black woolen robe with a well-fitting hood from beneath which his clear blue eyes looked out at the assembly, his long grey beard spilling down the front of his robe. Both Chris and Maxim, as well as Dean Killgower, made sure to visit with the wizened Elder during the allotted time, during which he questioned all three of them on certain points, which they promised to address in the ensuing discussion. Meanwhile Maria and Sophie were circulating among the tables, where their brothers joined them in time to touch base with their audience a bit before the Dean, after nearly a quarter of an hour, signaled the commencement of the concluding dialogue by chiming his empty glass with a spoon before refilling it from a pitcher that was itself freshly refilled. He began:

Rev. Dr. Killgower: Dearly beloved, we have gleaned by brief discussion with a number of you, a set of points on which further discussion would be appreciated. To begin with, clarification is requested regarding the "intellectual order of the disciplines" by which the order of our speakers was determined. On this point I have asked our Metaphysicals to respond in turn.

Maxim: St. John of Damascus, after defining true philosophy as the love of God, considers it as divided into practical and speculative sciences, and further divides the latter into theology, physiology or physics, and mathematics. Theology, he said, considers "incorporeal and immaterial things"—God above all, then "angels and souls". Physiology or physics is concerned with "material things" and their motions, and mathematics with things "in themselves incorporeal" which yet are "found in corporeal beings". In this view, theology is clearly the higher or prior science, subsuming even metaphysics, as well as psychology in the traditional sense. In Christian theology, it is of course the divine revelation that is definitive for the discipline, above and beyond the considerations of natural philosophy.

Christopher: The Damascene's division of the sciences likely derives from Aristotle's, which it exactly matches, and which calls the "highest science" theology because, as the Philosopher put it, "if the divine is present anywhere, it is present in things of this sort", that is, things "incorporeal" and "immaterial". As for Aquinas, there was no doubt in his mind that theology, which he called *sacra doctrina*, supersedes philosophy as such, precisely by the factor mentioned by Max, namely divine revelation in Holy Scripture, which is the very Principle of theology, as Johann Gerhard put it. And speaking for myself, as the metaphysician on deck, I heartily concur that theology precedes metaphysics in intellectual order, just as the divine Intellect precedes the human intellect created in its image.

Maria: A beautiful analogy, brother! And I, in turn, as the mathematician "on deck", most willingly concede the priority of metaphysics, itself subordinate to theology, to the science of numbers and forms that has bedazzled me since girlhood. After all, the mathematical objects or *mathemata* that we study, whatever they are, are surely created forms deriving from uncreated precursors in the Creator, and the question of what the *mathemata* really are, to which I just alluded, is really a metaphysical question. So *nolo contendere* on my part, for the placement of my science.

Sophia: What then can your humble astronomer do, along with your humble linguist, but fall gracefully in line behind the sciences of God, of intelligible being and reality, and of numbers and forms that are virtually constitutive of created nature as we observe it. While my twin brother was fantasizing about being a desert hermit and painter of icons, and my dear friend Chris was wandering and wondering about the greenwood, daydreaming about the reality of things, and my soul sister Maria was proving theorems on envelopes and napkins, I was staying up at night to gaze into space, or on cloudy nights, translating little snippets of text between Russian, Spanish, and English. Formally speaking, astronomy is concerned with corporeal objects in spacetime and their motions, which are created by God as metaphysically intelligible and mathematically representable: therefore astronomy presupposes theology, metaphysics, and mathematics. The same logic applies to linguistics, which is concerned with a class of intelligible structures employed for semantic communication by created intellects.

Rev. Dr. Killgower: Splendid! Thank you all very much. But before we move on to our next topic I must pose a small question to each of the ladies. Beginning with Maria then: Will you kindly elaborate a little on the "question of what the *mathemata* really are", to which you have twice merely alluded?

Maria: I shall do my best, dear Reverend Doctor, to address your excellent question, which according to my learned brother, Aristotle himself was initially unsure of, namely, whether the objects of mathematics are "immovable" as God is and "separable from matter", or whether they exist only as "embodied in matter". But having said the point was "not at present clear", the Philosopher goes on to state that the *mathemata* "presumably do not exist separately", which becomes his settled view. As St. Thomas puts it, "mathematics does not consider things which are separable from matter in being, but only in their intelligible structure". In other words, the *mathemata* do not really exist apart from their embodiment in sensible matter. But this is debatable, as my dear Maxim can attest, or even any true-blue Augustinian—since the Eastern view is that our spiritual intellect can access the uncreated *logoi* in God, and Augustine held that we have intellection of created ideas or *rationes* deriving from precursors in God. Personally, let me just say I am no Aristotelian on this point, which I hope to have illuminated at least a little.

Rev. Dr. Killgower: Thank you my dear! Well and delightfully done for a "mere" mathematician! Sometimes I think the four of you breathe metaphysics instead of air. And now a question for our astronomer: Sophia, will you please clarify your earlier description of galaxies and gamma-ray bursts in deep space?

Sophia: Maybe I skipped over that too quickly. It's really a pretty simple point, although I'm not sure it has been fully integrated into creation cosmology. Remember, this was one of the examples I gave of astronomical evidence for Earth as the center of the universe, along with the super-galactic "fingers of God" pointing toward Earth from all directions, and the alignments of the deep-space microwave structure with Earth's orbit. The point in question is simply that, looking into deep space from Earth in the gamma-ray spectrum, we see localized bursts of radiation (GRBs) originating from the farthest reaches of observable spacetime and almost invariably, between the Earth and the GRB lies a galaxy, so that the GRB and the galaxy form a line pointing straight at earth. Again, I offer this only as evidence that the universe is geocentric, without pretending to a full theoretical treatment. Does that help?

Rev. Dr. Killgower: Yes, I do believe it does. Thank you, my dear. And now I invite your attention to another topic, condensed from a variety of comments and questions from our friends here assembled. In short, I invite you to correlate the notion of creation by divine knowledge (CDK), which was touched on in the discourses of the gentlemen, with the geocentric white-hole (GWH) cosmology that was unveiled by the ladies. Please feel free to respond as the Spirit moves.

Maxim: According to my name-saint, the Confessor, every created being derives from an uncreated *logos* comprised within the divine *Logos*, who was in the beginning with God, and who was God. These *logoi* are the intellectual intentions of the Creator to create precisely the corresponding creatures. So creation begins with God's knowledge of the creatures, and the unity of creation is assured by the unity of the divine *Logos*, who is the Second Person of the Holy Trinity.

Christopher: St. Thomas puts it bluntly: "The knowledge of God is the cause of things." Since God's omniscience is infallible, if He knows something to exist it must really exist. And since the nature or essence of every created being, which makes it *what* it is, derives directly from its idea or *ratio* in God, by which the creature is known to God before its creation, it follows that God's creation of a creature is essentially His knowledge of the creature and of His will that it exist. As Thomas puts it, "it is manifest that God causes things by His intellect, since His being is His act of understanding, and so His knowledge must be the cause of things, insofar as His will is joined to it."

Maria: So we begin with God's eternal foreknowledge of creation, His direct epistemological contact with every finite location in spacetime from alpha to omega, both as prefigured eternally in Himself and as actually existing by His will. Now suppose that God understands the creation to originate as a vast globular abyss of pure water, subject to His physical laws of interaction—gravitational, electromagnetic, and nuclear—all regulated by the most elegant mathematical equations. Suppose further that God knows just when to alter the cosmological coefficient He has built into the mathematics, in order to switch the black-hole collapse of the cosmic abyss to a white-hole expansion, stretching spacetime itself and accelerating time at large distances from the center.

Sophia: "The heavens declare the glory of God, and the firmament proclaims His handiwork." When Holy Scripture declares the creation of the heavens and the firmament, it does so from a distinctly geocentric point of view, which we have seen to be supported by astronomical data as well. The class of cosmologies known as GWH do indeed solve the problem of a young Earth and ancient stars, and the aqueous origin with initial polarization explains the celestial magnetic fields. Remarkable correlations have been made between the order of the Six Days as narrated in Genesis, the deepest layers of the geologic record, and nucleosynthesis of the terrestrial elements in GWH perspective.

Have we really achieved a true understanding, so far as our finite minds can manage, or even perhaps an intellectual inkling of how God brought it all to be? Or rather, has God permitted us to participate in His knowledge of how it was done? God only knows!

Rev. Dr. Killgower: Bravo all! A well-spoken *ad libitum* (though I saw a few note-cards exchanged). But now the evening is well advanced, and our day has been an eventful one, from our morning Baccaleureate service, according to the Rite of St. Tikhon, with our beloved Elder presiding and your humble servant preaching, through the afternoon entertainments and the Graduation ceremony, through this Valedictory Symposium which you all have been moved to attend. It is therefore time to think about drawing these delightful discourses to a close, except for one final topic that remains to be addressed. Elder Lavrenty would like to know the reason or intention of Christopher's pursuit of the "technical speculations" he has mentioned. Specifically it occurs to the Elder that Christopher may be contemplating space travel, and he wonders if Christopher thinks he can escape the End of Time! There it is, Mr. Eckhart: the floor is yours.

Christopher: I salute the perspicacity of the venerable Elder as to the general drift of my project to design an ontological drive system for trans-physical teleportation, as well as ontological insulation of a teleportable vessel. Designing and building model spaceships from a variety of materials has been an avocation of mine from boyhood, so I suppose it's sort of a natural development. But no, I harbor no illusions about escaping the End, since I assume the whole geocentric universe will be "dissolved in fire" as St. Peter puts it, along with this Earth, at that juncture. Of course I differ from my mentor Aquinas on this point, which may be what prompted the question. In the standard cosmology of Thomas' time the astronomical heavens were considered identical with the metaphysical, spiritual heavens, home to angelic and human spirits. Therefore he thought the stars were of incorruptible matter and would not be involved in the refining fire at Christ's return. Today we consider the stars as distant corporeal objects containing chemical elements known on earth and subject to the same physical laws, as distinct from the metaphysical firmament of created spirits— even though the two orders overlap, as in Sophie's hypothesis. Therefore I figure the stars will dissolve in fire along with the Earth. On the other hand though, I guess the celestial bodies would also undergo the metaphysical transposition into the new heavens surrounding the new Earth—but we won't need spaceships to visit them, not in our new spiritual bodies. To be honest, I don't have any particular voyage in mind. But maybe there's a reason I'm not aware of yet, behind the inclination to pursue this.

Elder Lavrenty: Perhaps there is, my son. Perhaps there is. In any case, I am at peace with your answer.

With that, Dean Killgower rose in his position to one side of our Metaphysicals at table, a picturesque figure in his large tartan jacket, especially against the background of the emblematic painting of the metaphysical Ox and the evangelical Swan, centered on the great golden Bible. As was his custom, he raised an empty glass for his final toast, to the two illustrious Doctors behind him, the four brilliant Baccalaureates beside him, and the whole assembly of friends who had listened intelligently to their discourses. With the valedictory Symposium thus formally ended, the audience mingled momentarily with the Metaphysicals, and gradually dissolved into the night, followed by the Elder and the Dean. Chris and Sophia left the Ox & Swan hand in hand, as did Max and Maria.

CHAPTER TWO:
THE TRIENNIAL INTERIM

I.

On the morning after their valedictory appearance, the four friends met in the outdoor courtyard of the College Cafe for breakfast. There, over yogurt and granola, *huevos rancheros*, and plenty of strong coffee, our Metaphysicals shared a leisurely conversation concerning their immediate future. Later that day the Lossky-Mendez twins would depart for the family ranch in Texas while the Eckharts returned to their farm. In about six weeks Maria would visit the Texans at their ranch, from which she and Sophie would head north to graduate school in the Rockies to get settled in for the term. Chris would be busy with farm work until after the harvest, but he would find time to retreat to his study, walled off at one end of a hayloft, to pursue the intellectual quest that destiny had offered him. And Max would help out around the ranch until after the girls headed north, then move to the Seminary nearby to pursue his own studies. That much was all very simple, however long they lingered over the details. But what air of wistfulness descended almost tangibly over their table as the time for departure drew nigh?

The attentive reader will have observed that, in addition to the relation of twinship, another kind of relation was operative in this quartet of characters, namely that Max and Maria, Chris and Sophia, were lovers, although chastely. And this matter of chastity was by no means incidental to their romance, for all four of them had prayed and pondered hard over it, and both couples had mutually agreed to confine their lovemaking to hugs and kisses. But the matter did not end there, for the question of chastity did not pertain, for these young Christians, merely to their premarital life. For them the End of Time was only decades away, though they knew not the day nor the hour, and so the additional burden was laid upon them, to consider whether they should marry and bear children at all.

That their love was genuine, in the sense that under normal conditions they would inevitably marry and raise families, was indubitable to their hearts. But that they should bear children to live through the great tribulation preceding the Lord's return, was not yet obvious to them. So the archetypal wistfulness of lovers about to part was further heightened by the uncertainty whether the conjugal unions of their dreams would ever actually be consummated. Also, above and beyond this common ambivalence about bearing children at the End of Time, Maxim had long been attracted to an eremitic ideal of the spiritual life which included celibacy. The Orthodox church allowed its priests to choose either celibacy or marriage, and until he had met Maria, Max had been fairly sure he wouldn't marry. With Maria, however, he could for the first time very much imagine marriage.

The four have given themselves three years to pursue their studies and to ponder the question of matrimony. In the interim they will write to one another, perhaps meeting on major holidays now and then. We shall follow them largely by way of excerpts from this correspondence, tied together by such narrative as proves essential. But before we turn to the first letter, let us cast a quick glance at the two family estates to which the respective twins were departing. The Eckhart farm, located on the Appalachian Plateau in western Pennsylvania, not too far from New Bethlehem, covered roughly two hundred acres of cropland, of which half was in grass and the other half divided between oats, wheat, barley, corn and beans. The grasslands provided hay and grazing for a herd of grassfed beef cattle, and the other crops fed the chickens and/or were sold as surplus, as indeed a substantial garden plot fed the family. There were also around thirty acres of woodland on the property. The white farmhouse and the red barn and outbuildings were well maintained, and the pair of midsize tractors and other equipment by which the Eckharts worked the fields were securely sheltered.

By contrast, the Lossky-Mendez ranch occupied some five hundred acres in the Texas Hill Country, in the eastern part of the Edwards Plateau, sixty miles south of San Angelo.

The acreage was entirely in pasture and browse for a herd of sheep and goats, managed primarily by a foreman retained by Maxim's father, a professor of Russian literature. Besides the neat and sturdy ranch house there was a stable for the horses used in herding the flocks, and a more elaborate system of paddocks and fencing, constructed of ground-hugging grid-wire, than the Eckharts required for their cattle. Known to the family as the "Lucky M", this little ranch in Texas held precious memories for Max and Sophie, as did the Pennsylvania farm for their romantic partners.

Among the most precious of Maxim's memories were Maria's previous visits to the Lucky M over the past several years, and this summer's stay during the latter part of July was no exception. Maria loved being on horseback, and Max had been riding since he was little, so the two of them shared many hours riding the range together, watching the flocks, conversing and not conversing. But the allotted weeks passed by quickly, and the first days of August saw the two young women, ready for their next round of studies, all set to embark. After seeing off his sister and his lover, and bidding farewell to his parents, Max took his bags and made his way to Seminary, from which a couple of weeks later he mailed the following letter to the other three.

August 13 2040 A.D.
Feast of St. Maximus Confessor

Dearly Beloved,

The Spirit has moved me to commence our formal correspondence on this festal day, as I settle into Seminary and prepare for the oncoming term. I've been working my *tschotki* pretty hard, trying to stay centered in the Jesus Prayer for spiritual preparation, while entertaining fond memories of our time together at College, and since. Remarkable how we gravitated together almost at once, Chris and I, Sophie and Maria, and then our other affections blossoming so quickly, our reputation as a formidable foursome already formed by our sophomore year, and crowned with our inimitable moniker by old Lewis, the Brit Lit man. So many hours of conversation in the Ox & Swan and elsewhere, unforgettable moments alone with Maria, wondering and praying what the future held for us, and here we are pursuing that very future.

I sense more strongly than ever that God has a mission for us, that our corresponding *logoi* in Him stand in a kind of harmonic relation to each other, so that our activities in this life are predestined to be coordinated. Call it a prophecy, call it a hunch. In any case, I would like to celebrate the Feast of my name-saint with a little discourse on his Christocentric vision of the created universe, in which every existing creature expresses an uncreated *logos* within the eternal *Logos*, namely the Son of God. In one sense all created beings are One in Christ, since their corresponding *logoi*, the principles of their existence, are comprised in Him "undivided and unconfused"— as is also said of the two natures of Christ in His personal unity. The exquisite formal precision and coordination of activities exhibited in the created universe reflect the organization of the uncreated *logoi* in Christ. The *logos* of every creature is the very core of its being, but because this *logos* is uncreated it is never confused with the creature.

There are also divine energies, according to St. Maximus, which are *distinct* from the divine Essence but *not separate*, and which therefore are uncreated like the Essence, but which created beings can participate in according to the specifications of their *logoi*. It is notable that both the *logoi* and the divine energies (or activities) have the property of being uncreated (i.e., in God), and yet present at the core of every creature, or available to the creature by participation. The participation of the creatures in the energies is regulated by God's organization of the *logoi* in Christ. And lastly, the *logos* of a creature means not only its principle of origin but its goal, its pole-star as it were, during its temporal lifetime, according to which it should live as intended by God, and achieve final well-being in eternity. Amen.

But this brings me back to where I started, with sheer wonder at the phenomenon of the four of us, and wondering especially what God has in mind. For now, the best I can do is to keep the ball rolling by offering a couple of thoughts on your respective studies, which occur to me when I think of you. Christopher's quest for metaphysical precursors of physical processes will surely involve the *logoi*, or whatever Latin equivalent he might prefer, but these are in God, after all, which means his teleportation technology will require *divine action*. Indeed, if he is given this invention, it will be tantamount to a miracle. My star-struck sister's reconnaissance of starlight for signs of angelic language will certainly involve the play of *logoi* and energies, both in her own intellectual life and in the starlight itself, whether or not it is modulated by angels. And my dearest Maria's investigations into mathematical forms and structures are directed to concrete intelligible objects which, however one locates them ontologically, derive from *logoi* contained in the Logos, our Lord Jesus Christ.

Not much to tell about Seminary yet. I have a small single room with a view of St. John's Chapel across the campus, and there's a great running trail along the river. Other students are still moving into the dorm, so I've helped carry a few boxes but haven't really had a serious chat with anyone yet. I miss you all.

Keep the faith, fight the good fight, let your light

shine. Beware of the evil one. I send you all a holy
kiss.

In Christ,

Maxim

The letter was dispatched electronically, and while Chris
and Sophia received it gladly and read it with care (he in
his *studium* in the loft and she by her windows on the sky),
it was Maria of course whose heart was stirred to respond,
and quickly. Indeed, she had already been thinking of
inaugurating the correspondence herself, on the Feast
of her own name-saint, when Max's epistle had arrived.
Accordingly, she wrote:

August 15, 2040 A.D.
Feast of St. Mary

Dearest Maxim, Christopher my brother,
Sophia my friend and colleague,

I report on behalf of Sophie, who will write in
a month or so, that she and I are settled into a
modest double room at Creation A&M. In the
short time before classes begin we are getting the
lay of the land, with the help of a riding stable with
reasonable rentals. Also scoping out the Library
and Supercomputing Center, and of course the

Observatory, as well as meeting some of the faculty we hope to work with.

I want to follow Max's lead by offering a little festal discourse for St. Mary, Santa Maria, the Mother of God, whose *soul magnified the greatness of the Lord* (not so far as His unchangeable nature is concerned, as Luther says, but in the knowledge that esteems Him above self); and whose *spirit rejoiced in God our Savior* (spirit being the "highest, deepest, and noblest part" of human being, according to Luther, by which we can "lay hold of things incomprehensible, invisible, eternal", and which is the "dwelling place of faith and the Word of God". Now our Lady sings that she *rejoiced* in her spirit, in God, using the same Greek verb by which Jesus *rejoiced* in the Holy Spirit according to St. Luke; for into our spirit, which is our spiritual "heart", come faith and the Word of God, meaning Christ with the Holy Spirit, so that the eternal joy of the Holy Spirit actually abides in us! The Lord truly *looks with favor* on all whom He has *called blessed* by this faith, *having mercy on us who fear Him*. Let us not be *proud in the conceit of our hearts* so that He need not *scatter* us, but let us be *lowly* so that He may *lift us up*. Let us trust in His *promise of mercy*, and give thanks to the Lord, for He is good.

In His mercy He has given us also Geometry, my great intellectual love since girlhood, and a science on which I have been pondering much these days—not surprisingly since I now seek a doctorate therein. My brother has persuaded me to maintain a Thomist view of my science, and therefore to dismiss the non-Euclidean experiments as being outside the subject of Geometry proper, which is quantitative being, or intelligible substance subject to quantity. The objects of Geometry are continuous, quantified substances in which intelligible matter is quantitatively formed by indivisible boundaries (points in a line, lines in a plane, planes in a solid). An interesting corollary of this view is that quasi-Einsteinian geometrodynamic theories of matter and energy in spacetime, are not describing geometrical objects but physical ones—as in GWH cosmologies, where spacetime, matter, energy and all are thought of as being stretched rapidly away from Earth.

Sticking to the real objects of Geometry then, since these are intelligible substances with quantitative being, they really exist in some created mode, as knowable by created intellects, and so presumably, in Maximian terms, they also derive from uncreated *logoi* in Christ like all other created substances. I've actually been doing some daydreaming on the use of geometrical methods in looking for meaningful correlations between frequency bands in the structure of starlight, at various intervals of time and across the whole electromagnetic spectrum. But

I have to complete some heavy-duty coursework with several of the "heavies" in the mathematical faculty, before I'm ready to really team up with Sophie. The standing joke in our apartment is that the "A&M" in the name of the university stands for "Astronomical & Mathematical", not from any prejudice towards Agriculture and Mechanics (God forbid!) but because of the excellence of the faculties here in our own sciences.

I share Max's wonderment at the sheer "phenomenon of the four of us", not pridefully of course, since we have been given all of our gifts and each other too: all glory be to the Giver! May the Maker of all phenomena make of us what He will. God bless and keep you all,

In Christ,

Maria

According to the agreed protocol for their "formal" correspondence during the three-year interim, all four of our Metaphysicals were to write before any of them wrote again, so that the letters would fall into cycles of four. No definite order had been planned, so with Sophie just starting her first graduate term and Chris still in the thick of harvest, God only knew who would write next. The reader should be advised that certain private communications were occasionally exchanged between the siblings, and between the lovers, of which our narrative will respect the privacy, concentrating entirely on the letters they considered "formal". And the next of these, as it turned out, was from our astronomer and linguist, Sophia Lossky-Mendez.

September 14, 2040 A.D.
Exaltation of the Holy Cross

Christopher my love, Maxim my brother,
Maria my roommate and colleague,

The Lord be with you.

The absence of my mathematician at an evening seminar in differential geometry, along with my own preparedness as to assignments for tomorrow's classes, leaves me alone in the apartment, with a fine view of the northern sky and time to write this letter. Also it happens to be a holy day (I attended Divine Liturgy earlier), so I can date it by the liturgical calendar like Max and Maria did. Thus I am sitting at my desk on the Feast of the Holy Cross, and looking out the window at the northern sky, when what do I spy but Cygnus the Swan, otherwise known as the Northern Cross, right in the center of my view! In keeping with the precedent of briefly celebrating the sacred theme of the day, I therefore lift up the Cross of our Lord Jesus Christ, upon which He sacrificed Himself for the sin of the fallen creation, so that by His blessed Resurrection

He might open to us the Way of eternal Life. And so I celebrate the astronomical legend of the Swan of the Cross, which unites the two names of the fabled constellation that overlooks me as I write, and which identifies our Lord as the dying Swan whose song is our life and salvation. In particular His long, final discourse in the Gospel of John, culminating in the high-priestly prayer of chapter 17, has been referred to as His swan song in this connection. Alleuia to Jesus, the Swan of the Cross! May He keep us in the shelter of His wings!

The past month has been busy and stimulating, both in preparation for the term to begin and in the first weeks of classes. I've been spending a lot of time around the Observatory, talking with staff and getting familiar in a general way with the optical telescopes, including the big reflector, as well as the radio, x-ray, and gamma-ray equipment. I'm in a fantastic seminar in stellar photometry which covers the whole range of techniques for the measurement and analysis of starlight, and recently a special lecture summarized the current observational data on the "fingers of God" I mentioned in our Symposium. First of all there is no longer any question about the reality of the observed supergalactic structures, as opposed to hypotheses that they were somehow artifacts of the observational technique. Secondly, the ongoing deep-space survey of our sky, with refinements of the basic technique pioneered in the

1970's, continues to confirm the existence of linear filaments of galaxies pointing toward Earth.

On the linguistics front I am studying with perhaps the greatest living Christian grammarian, who has done work both with Luther's "grammar of the Holy Spirit" operative in Scripture, and with Maximus Confessor's theory of *logoi*! I believe he is a bit bemused by my project, though not exactly negative. When he sees how I master his material (Lord willing), I think he'll come around. So here are a few preliminary musings for y'all. Since the angelic intellect does not know by means of language as we do, there would be no angelic dialect per se. But what if the angels associated with the stars (or some of them) proceeded to *express* their knowledge, perhaps in hymns of praise, perhaps in prophecy, so as to be intelligible to light-sensitive intellectual beings who are distant in spacetime from the stars associated with these angels? Wouldn't such angelic communications exhibit universal characteristics of grammar? Then they would contain discrete units of *meaning*, signified by articulated *physical vibrations*, and arranged in a *syntactic structure*. Classically the articulate vibrations are of sound (phononic); in this case they are of light (photonic). Like Maria, I have some heavy coursework to do before refining this hypothesis.

Speaking of Maria, here she is (here you are) back

from the seminar, eyes all atwinkle! That's about enough for one letter anyway. I'm looking at the Swan of the Cross in the northern sky, and sending you His light with these words.

In Christ,

Sophia

The onus of the correspondence had now fallen clearly upon Christopher Eckhart, who after all had made known his preoccupation, but who had by no means been out of touch privately with his lady. As September gave way to October, everything was in but the corn, and that was only a matter of a week or ten days, including the roasting, grinding and blending of some of the corn, beans and grains to make feed for the chickens. Later in the fall he and his dad would be cutting some firewood, of which they used a modest amount for heating to supplement the cheap Pennsylvania natural gas, which they used for part of the heating and to run the tractors. Farmer Eckhart also had a small sawmill by which they provided any necessary lumber by careful timbering of the wooded acreage, and also sawed for neighbors, again in the late fall. But the middle of October was looking like a nice little breather in which he might fulfill his epistolary obligation. And such indeed turned out to be the case.

October 18, 2040 A.D.
Feast of St. Luke

Beloved Sophia, sister Maria, soul-brother Maxim,

Grace to you and peace.

In keeping with the precedent you have established, I date this on the Festival of St. Luke the Evangelist, St. Paul's "beloved physician", in whose honor I offer the following *meditatio* on several verses from his Gospel. Maria mentions the rejoicing of Jesus reported in verse 10:21, where the same Greek verb is used for His "rejoicing" as is used for St. Mary's rejoicing in verse 1:47, her Magnificat. In this parallel, Jesus rejoices in the Holy Spirit and Mary's spirit rejoices in God. Now right before this rejoicing of Jesus, according to St. Luke, He had told His disciples to "rejoice that your names are written in heaven" (10:20b) But here the Greek verb that the KJV translates "rejoice" is a different verb, namely the one that the angel Gabriel used to address St. Mary (Luke 1:28), which is there translated "Hail". So an alternative translation of the angel's address would be "Rejoice, Mary". So in this parallel, Jesus tells us to rejoice that our names are written in heaven, as Gabriel told St. Mary to rejoice that the Lord was with her. In sum: St. Luke uses the same verb to signify Jesus' rejoicing in the Holy Spirit and Mary's spirit rejoicing in God; but uses a different verb to signify both the rejoicing commended to Mary by Gabriel regarding her conception of Jesus, and the rejoicing commended by Jesus to those whose names are written in heaven. I infer that Jesus' rejoicing in the Third Person of His own divine nature involved the spiritual part of his human nature, just as Mary's rejoicing in God our Savior involved the spiritual part of her nature; and that having our names written in heaven involves the conception of the Word in our spiritual parts (hearts).

I hope Max in particular will excuse these exegetical efforts of an amateur theologian, and a Lutheran at that! Also I appreciate the good counsel, from the same quarter, regarding the dependency of an ontological teleportation technology upon divine action—divine energies if you will. This is most certainly true. Whether or not the invention is a real possibility depends upon its being in accord with the will of God. But isn't this true of everything that comes into being? Even the most diabolical inventions of modern military technology could never have existed except for the permission of His will, allowing the full character of the End Time to develop. Yet this invention will require more than the permission of God's will; it will require the active intervention thereof. So here's how I see it: I've prayed a lot over this, asking the Lord to just take this obsession away from me, withdraw all support and inspiration, and give me something else to think about—unless it is His will that I proceed. And still my thinking returns again and again to the theoretical foundations of ontological transposition, and my imagination teems with variations on the structure of a vessel (mingled with fond images of a certain fair astronomer). In other words, it still looks like a go.

As I told Elder Lavrenty at our valedictory, I have no particular voyage in mind. After all, the voyage would have to be part of the will of God empowering and energizing the technology, would it not? So the voyage, or mission, and the technology to carry it out, would be aspects of God's particular plan in this matter, which would preexist as ideas or *logoi* in *Christus Intellectus*, would they not? And the assignment of *esse* to these preexistent ideas, according to the will of God, would produce the actual existence of the technology and the voyage it makes possible. Q.E.D., right? So the quest is on. I was especially struck by Maria's clear declaration of the distinction between geometric objects per se, being purely mathematical, and any *physical* mapping of their structures into geometrodynamic spacetime. Thus the material character of physical spacetime, of which matter-energy is a "geometrical" property pertaining to the curvature of spacetime.

But let me wind this up with a bit of local color.

Summer was fairly hot, with just enough rain for the crops, so the harvest has been excellent! The haylofts are full, as are the corn cribs and granary bins. The steers are sleek and stocky, and the chickens are thriving. Thanks be to God! Oh! And Aunt Lucy visited from Philadelphia for two weeks. She and Mom sang their Afro-Italian hearts out doing Gospel duets and harmonizing hymns, while Dad and I hummed along as best we could.

Yes, well. That's about it, my dear ones. May the Lord lift up His countenance upon you, and give you peace,

In Christ,

Christopher

II.

The fall term passed quickly for the seminarian and the two grad students, filled as it was with challenging and stimulating coursework, while the metaphysical farmer wound up the activities of autumn and found more time for his studies. Sophie and Maria stayed at school over Thanksgiving, hosting a small group of friends for the day, and their brothers manned the home front, carving turkey with their respective parents. At Christmastide both of the sisters returned to their families for just over a week, but the lovers had decided not to see each other over break, however much their private communications may have intensified during that time. In any case, the four were soon preoccupied with their winter studies, when it was Max once again who opened the second cycle of correspondence.

March 7, 2041 A.D.
Feast of St. Thomas Aquinas

Dearly beloved,

I greet you on the festal day of Christopher's blessed patron, whose insistence on the supreme authority of Scripture was unerring, and whose Christian interpretation of Greek metaphysics was a great gift to the Church. Grace to you, and peace.

I must tell you right away the main reason I am writing today, namely a waking vision I saw just before dawn this morning. I'd awakened earlier than usual, so I got up and prayed my *tschotki*, then headed out of the dorm for a run on the river trail. It was just after five A.M. Suddenly there was something like a flash of light in the sky, and when I turned in the direction of the apparent flash I found myself looking directly at Cygnus the Swan! I didn't have long to ponder the meaning of that, when all at once I saw the *Swan*, a pale white Swan covering the constellation. In the middle of the

Swan's back, an orb of brighter light enshrined the Christ Child! But not only that! Swiftly the wings of the great Swan became twelve wings, distributed among three angels and a six-winged seraph. The three angels stood above and to each side of the Child, and the seraph stooped below Him like a throne, just as in the icon called the Synaxis of the Angels, and still superimposed on the constellation! Then, in the next instant, I was seeing only the stars again. So what do y'all make of that?

Here are some of my reflections: First there is the one-to-one correspondence between the five major stars of Cygnus and the five figures of the icon. If we take the figures as symbolizing the ruling spirits of the corresponding stars, this would set the central and bottom stars apart from the other three, since the latter spirit would be a six-winged seraph, and the former would be Christ Himself! The next thing that occurs to me is whether this vision, in the wake of Sophie's paean to the Swan of the Cross last September, pertains not only to the work of Sophie and Maria, as to which stars to start with, but also to the unanswered question of where Christopher's space ship is to go. Perhaps I am jumping to conclusions, and only time will tell (though God already knows), but I can tell you the vision really got my attention. If I close my eyes I can still see the radiant orb enshrining the Child, on the back of the great pale Swan, then the three angels and the seraph, all superimposed upon the stars of Cygnus! Anyway, the other connection that occurs to me is between the four stars around the central star, or the four angelic beings around the Christ Child, and the four of us grouped around whatever purpose or mission the Lord has in mind for us—or around the Lord Himself.

That's about all on the vision per se. I've been thinking about it all day, right though my classes in Bible and Patristics and an afternoon seminar on St. Maximus, where I couldn't help seeing it through the lens of the *logoi*. Thus: each of the five major stars, as a created corporeal being, must have its *logos* in Christ; each of the five corresponding angels (per Sophie's Thomist theory), as a created spiritual being, likewise. Now in the vision the central star comes to symbolize Christ Himself, although it may be doubted whether Christ is actually the moving spirit of that star, since He contains the *logoi* of all stars, and of everything else. In the connection with the four of us, the four *logoi* from which we derive our being become part of the equation, or matrix: fifteen *logoi* in three ranks, five astronomic, five angelic, and four human with Christ in our midst, human nature and all (as in Divine Liturgy).

It seems I am unable to write about anything but the vision tonight, and I've written about all I should for now. So I'll just respond quickly to a technical point from Christopher's letter, and then wrap this one up. Equating a Thomist notion of uncreated ideas with the Maximian *logoi*, he asks rhetorically whether these would not preexist in Christ as Intellect of the Trinity, which I agreeably affirm. But his statement following refers to the "assignment of *esse* to these preexistent ideas" in order to "produce the(ir) actual existence," which would not necessarily apply to the *logoi*, in the sense that these are conceived by the Confessor as containing in themselves an intrinsic will of God to their actualization. Perhaps this will be helpful in Christopher's quest, in which I wish him Godspeed, as also to my sister and to my lady in theirs.

Winter has been mild down here: just enough rain, no major storms. Nothing to compare with the Rockies or western Pennsylvania, that's for sure. The routine here has been good for me, though I keep seeing a certain pair of bright blue eyes in my dreams. I can definitely say that my priestly vocation is being confirmed, and I can also report that several of the priests on faculty, including the Seminary chaplain, whom I believe to be very spiritual men, appear to be very happily married. On that note, I send you the peace of God which passes all understanding, that it may keep your hearts and your minds,

In Christ,

Maxim

No one made haste, this time, to reply. Maria and Sophie were hard at work finishing out their first year at Creation A&M, preparing for exams and presentations, and grading papers for their teaching-assistant requirements. Chris too was bearing down on his metaphysical studies, and by April and May he was already into the spring manuring, plowing and planting, as well as the first cutting of hay. On top of all that, he enjoyed a ten-day visit from his lady, who visited the Eckhart farm at the end of their term, after which the two young ladies continued together to the Lucky M, for a visit of similar length. This gave both pairs of lovers some much-awaited time for such tender assurances of affection as can only occur face to face. It also gave Sophie a chance to see her dirt-farmer in action, his muscles pumped from handling bales of hay, his sweat-drenched, suntanned face covered with chaff, his dark blue eyes giving her that look. She wouldn't have minded pitching in, but mom Eckhart wanted the girls' help with spring cleaning, harvesting from the kitchen garden, cooking, and just filling her in on their lives—her daughter and (hopefully) daughter-in-law—which was pleasant enough after all. She'd managed to spend plenty of time with Chris, as Maria got to spend days riding with Max, watching the flocks, the landscape, and the sky. By a week into June, however, both of these lovers' trysts had transpired and passed, and the two travelers returned to the Rockies, Maria to teach undergraduate math tutorials and Sophie to work as a technician in the Observatory, paid from a grant secured by one of the astronomers on faculty. And it was at this point, that it turned out to be Maria again who wrote next.

June 24, 2041 A.D.
Feast of St. John the Baptist

Dearest Maxim, Christopher my brother,
Sophia my colleague and friend,

Festal greetings on the day of St. John the Fore-runner, called by our Lord the greatest man ever born of woman, and identified by Him as the "Elias" or Elijah who went before the "Lamb of God who takes away the sin of the world". This was in reference to Malachi's prophecy that Elias would precede the coming of the Christ. In other words, the Baptist played the Eliatic role in Christ's first coming, as the Eliatic Restoration to which we witness in our time apparently foreshadows His second, although Elias and Enoch have not yet shown themselves. Blessed be St. John the Baptist, the Eliatic Forerunner of our Lord Jesus Christ! And blessed be the Eliatic works that God is working in us! Amen.

What is uppermost in my mind and heart as I sit down to this letter, is the remarkable vision reported by my Maxim, over which I have been marveling and pondering for more than three months. To begin with, I can definitely confirm that Sophie and I will be focusing on those five stars for our initial studies. In fact she is spending the summer gathering data on their electromagnetic spectra, visible starlight included, while I narrow down the geometric methods available for the analysis of that data. We may have some preliminary results by the end of summer. But my sheer amazement at the vision goes far beyond this practical indication, right to the iconic character of the vision, and the way it ties into us. Max sent me a print of the Synaxis icon: the Holy Child in the center, orbed in light and seated on a six-winged seraph, with three adjacent angels left, right, and above Him, and seven more angels in the background, all robed in gold and celestial blue. The beauty of it moved me to tears the first time I looked at it!

Anyway, on Max's connection of the vision with us, here's a thought on why one of the four figures is different, the one in question being a seraph *on which Christ is enthroned*. Now the literal meaning of my brother's name is "Christ-bearer", and the seraph in the icon is literally "bearing Christ" in the manner of a seat. I have no thoughts, by the way, on why my brother would have as many "wings" as the rest of us put together, but I wanted to share the connection which occurred to me.

And speaking of Christopher, since returning to school I've had a couple of intuitive moments, in the course of my geometrical musings, that may be of use to his project. The first occurred in my review of the solid geometry of polyhedrons for one of my tutorials, when I came across a couple of pages of 2D projections of the regular and semiregular polyhedrons. Suddenly, I thought to myself, I wonder if Chris has considered a spherical vessel formed of nested polyhedrons? So there it is. See if it makes any sense to you, brother mine. The other thought came from, of all things, a lecture in crystallography I recently attended. We geometers were alerted because the class of crystals discussed in the lecture require more than 3D to describe their lattice structure: i.e., these "supercrystals" appear to be 3D "cross-sections" of a 4D or 5D crystalline lattice in superspace! Again I thought, I wonder if these are on Chris's radar? So that's it: a formal suggestion and a material suggestion. What more can a poor mathematician do?

I am blessed with a good group of tutorial students, really motivated and a pleasure to work with. Also there is plenty of time to think about geometries of light and to go riding in the hills with Sophie, often simultaneously. In closing, I would like to give thanks to the Lord for the happy marriages of my Maxim's professors, and to wish him a blessed summer, as also to my dear brother,

In Christ,

Maria

It was now full summer. The manuring, tilling, and plantings of spring now yielded the annual sequence of harvests—hay, barley, oats, wheat, hay again, beans, corn—and our metaphysical farmer, his spirit refreshed by his lady's visit and his sister's letter, had his work cut out for him until fall. Our theologian had been especially moved by Maria's letter, as much by her understanding of his vision as by her response to his mention of happy marriage, and he had many hours of keeping watch over the flocks during which to deeply ponder both. For he had decided to spend the summer working the Lucky M again, his advisor at Seminary having acknowledged with a smile that, after all, riding herd on flocks of sheep and of goats was hardly the worst preparation a man could have for being a pastor in the Church! Accordingly Maxim's profile, tall in the saddle, wiry but broad-shouldered, could often be seen on the high points and ridges overlooking the hillsides and hollows where the grazing or the browsing were best; while in close-up his quiet brown eyes, framed by his curly dark hair and beard, moved slowly over the landscapes of his beloved hill country. Meanwhile up north, in the Mountains, our "A&M" team managed to work some off-hour trail rides into their summer regimen, enjoying the austere majesty of the high Rockies amid their ongoing intellectual activities; Maria zeroing in on the geometrical methods she would bring to Sophie's data, and Sophia herself getting a head start and some background on their newly-acquired target constellation. Maria had more or less promised a preliminary report by late summer, and in view of her theme Sophie decided to write on the same date as before.

September 14, 2041 A.D.
Exaltation of the Holy Cross

Christopher my love, Maxim my brother,
Maria my dear mathematician,

Peace be with you. Glory to the Cross of our Lord Jesus Christ!

Again I am seated at my north-facing star window, and the stars of the Northern Cross shine down upon me as I write. I have long tended to envision the figure of the celestial Swan when I look at Cygnus, and even to genuflect at the image of the "Swan of the Cross". But after Max's vision I keep seeing the angels too, and the seraph, and the Child. I've always thought of astronomy as my sacred calling, but this takes it to a whole new level! So on that note I'll get right to the briefing y'all are probably expecting.

I've decided to focus on the five brightest stars (α-, β-, γ-, δ-, and ε-*Cygni*), which are in fact the five major stars of the Cross (and of the vision), as well as on one of the X-ray objects in the constellation, namely Cygnus X-3. So here's the roster:

α-*Cygni*, at the top of the Cross, is called Deneb, the "tail" (since the Swan is inverted); a blue supergiant appearing brilliant white at magnitude 1.4 (lower numbers meaning brighter), and apparently in motion directly toward Earth from about 1550 LYO (light years out).

β-*Cygni*, at the bottom of the Cross, is named Albireo, the "beak," and is really a binary system combining a golden yellow star of magnitude 3.5 with a sapphire blue star of magnitude 7, orbiting each other only 385 LYO.

γ-*Cygni* is the central star in the Cross, being named Sadr, the "breast," a golden-white star whose spectrum closely matches that of our Sun, its magnitude 2.7 at about 1525 LYO. Like Deneb it appears to be moving toward Earth.

δ-*Cygni*, marking the southeasterly arm of the Cross, is otherwise unnamed, being a trinary system comprising a blue-white giant, a smaller yellow-white star, and a dim orange star orbiting them at a distance, with a composite magnitude of 2.9 at about 171 LYO.

ε-*Cygni*, marking the northwesterly arm of the

Cross, is named Gienah, the "wing"; a single yellow star of magnitude 2.6, only around 72 LYO. I find it fascinating that α and γ are almost equidistant from Earth at just over 1500 LYO, while the other three are much closer to Earth, from 72 to 385 LYO. So if a certain metaphysician flew to Deneb, for example, and then to the other four stars in order, he would be jumping back and forth some 1200 LY and more, from distant to near, to distant, to near, to nearest. Moreover, I will be curious what he thinks of my illustration.

But I want to brief you also on the other object I mentioned, Cygnus X-3, which may be of great significance to us. More than 30 thousand LYO, X-3 was first discovered (1967) as a gamma-ray source, then in 1972 it produced a massive radio-frequency outburst which subsequently repeated every 367 days! Then in the early 1980's several deep-underground cosmic ray detectors picked up streams of particles from X-3, electrically neutral and travelling at near lightspeed, which did not fit the profile of any known physical particle. But these well-documented particles, called "cygnets" from their constellation of origin, suddenly ceased in October 1985, causing some to question their very existence. By the end of the 20th century, very-long-baseline radiotelescopy had detected in Cygnus X-3 a matter-energy jet of relativistic magnitude, aimed straight at Earth. The jet is powered by a binary system in which a large, matter-rich star is being consumed by a companion neutron star or black hole, emitting prodigious quantities of matter-energy quantized as radiofrequency, x-ray, gamma-ray, and cygnet rays (whatever they are). Not only is this axial relativistic jet aimed right toward Earth, it also happens to be close (in our sky) to γ-*Cygni*, Sadr, the center of the Cross, although it is more than 30 thousand LY further out. In other words, if you draw a line from Cygnus X-3 to Earth, it will pass near the central star. Fascinating.

So there's a basic briefing on some astronomical facts that may be pertinent to our mission. As for specific findings, I have amassed a mess of historical data for Maria, who has pretty well figured out her approach and is ready to take it to her advisor this term, to make the project official. Meanwhile, I will have much freer access to the telescopes this year for live studies, and will also formally advise my advisor of our intentions.

I wish you all a blessed autumn. From the Swan of the Cross, still shining faintly on my forehead as I write, I send you grace and peace,

In Christ,

Sophia

And a blessed autumn it was for our Metaphysicals. Settling into his second year at Seminary, Maxim established a daily routine that both celebrated his love of God and facilitated his theological studies. Rising early for prayer and a good run along the river, before Orthos, the service of morning prayer in St. John's chapel, and then morning classes in Scripture and Patristics, he had most afternoons free for quiet study, the exception being Wednesdays, when an after-lunch seminar on St. Maximus' *Ambigua* was followed by a two-hour lecture-workshop on the forms of the Divine Liturgy. Maxim's evenings consisted mostly of more study, punctuated however, several times a week, by chess matches with a group of worthy opponents he had found, giving him the opportunity to work on his game. Maria, while mastering the essential coursework for her degree, was happily trying out the geometric methods she had chosen for the linguistic analysis of starlight, on the historical data sets that Sophie had put together over the summer. Sophia meanwhile, with freer access to various instrumentation in the Observatory complex, was watching Cygnus like a hawk, or perhaps an owl, the ancient bird of wisdom; adding new observations visible and invisible, by night and by day, catching her sleep in the intervals, and of course acing her coursework. As for Christopher, the Eckhart farm had again yielded bountifully, keeping him busy into the fall, and there was extra sawmill activity due to a couple of local barn-raisings, wherefore it was not until two days after Christmas, with Maria already home for the holidays, that his long-awaited epistle was dated.

December 27, 2041 A.D.
Feast of St. John the Theologian

Sophia my sweetheart, Maria my sister,
Maxim my soul-brother,

The Lord be with you.

It is fitting that I sit down to write this report on the Feast of St. John the Theologian, author of the Gospel, the Epistles, and the visions of Revelation, because the thing that made me write just now is a vision I saw on Christmas Eve. It seems that my soul-brother is contagious, and at a distance! Anyway, here's what happened. I had been to the late Divine Service on Christmas Eve with the family, Maria included, and then warmed up my study for a late night. I knew this letter was overdue, but the synthesis I had been hoping for had not yet congealed intellectually, so I was reviewing and brooding over my notes and rereading all of your letters, including the extensive lines on Max's vision, when I heard behind me a small voice like a child's saying, "Draw what you see in a book, and use it as you are instructed."

Then I turned to see the voice that was speaking to me, and on turning I saw the Christ Child surrounded by an orb of radiance, like in the icon. Seated, He was about two feet tall, with a golden halo around His head. His face, though childlike, was grave and serene beyond His apparent age. In His left hand He held a scroll, and His right hand, which He held in front of His chest, formed the sign of His name. The orb of light in which he was seated was composed of three concentric spheres: the outermost a radiant white with starlike scintillations, the next one in a pale blue, and the innermost a deep blue against which the brilliant white rays streaming from the Child appeared clearly. He was barely fifteen feet away, toward the far end of my study, which was flooded with light. Despite the gravity of His countenance, the Child did not arouse fear in me, just an overwhelming sense of awe. I knelt on the floor and crossed myself.

Immediately the Christ Child disappeared, leaving the radiant orb with its concentric structure hovering before me. In the Child's absence I could see scintillations of white in the deep blue interior of the orb, each scintillation in the shape of the letter λ, which I somehow knew stood for λογοξ, (*logos*): in other words the deep blue core was sparkling with *logoi*. Suddenly a burst of rays emerged from these *logoi*, terminating at the boundary between the pale blue intermediate sphere and the outermost white one, and forming at that boundary the structure of a polyhedron, which I recognized as one of the semiregular or Archimedean polyhedrons that Maria had commended to my attention. But no sooner did I recognize this first polyhedron than a second burst of rays emerged from the *logoi* in the deep blue core to terminate at the outer boundary of the outermost white sphere, forming another polyhedron, which I also recognized. Remembering the voice, I quickly grabbed a notebook and began sketching enough of the two polyhedrons to confirm their identity, when now the vertices of the inner polyhedron, all twenty-four of them, flashed bright blue maybe six or seven times, and I heard the voice say, "4D supercrystals". While I was noting this on my rough sketch, the vertices of the outer polyhedron, no less than sixty this time, began flashing the same way as the voice said, "5D supercrystals." I was now sitting cross-legged on the floor facing the vision, so that I could hold the notebook.

The next thing I saw was the extension of a membrane or skin over the inner polyhedron, except over one of its square faces, while the voice whispered, "silicone-coated glass"; then the outer polyhedron likewise, but with "fluoropolymer-coated polyaramid," as the still small voiceover advised. This time it was one of the pentagonal faces which was left uncovered, with the surface membrane folded inside to meet the open square of the inner shell, making an entrance to the interior with hatches inside and out. The outer membrane, at this point, glowed with a beautiful celestial blue, and the name SYNAXIS appeared upon it in white; whereupon the hatches suddenly closed and the noble vessel, along with the vision that brought it, disappeared from my sight.

After praying and giving thanks to the Christ Child in the wee hours of His nativity, I spent the next several hours putting my diagrams, notes, and thoughts in order, and confirming the geometrical identities of the polyhedrons, as follows: The *inner* is called a "Rhombi-cubo-octahedron" and comprises eight equilateral triangles and eighteen squares, joined at forty-eight edges and twenty-four vertices; and the *outer* is a "Rhombi-icoso-dodecahedron" and comprises twenty equilateral triangles, thirty squares, and twelve pentagons, joined at 120 edges and sixty vertices. Notice that the -inner polyhedron consists of 3- and 4-sided faces and its vertices are set with 4-D supercrystals, while the outer polyhedron consists of 3-, 4-, and 5-sided faces, and its vertices are set with 5-D supercrystals, suggesting an inward to outward metaphysical gradient from 3-D to 5-D. Notice also that the vision didn't specify a material for the rods forming the edges of the polyhedrons, or how the two shells are connected, so I've got some thinking to do on those matters. Not to mention getting cost estimates for the technical membranes and finding a source for 4- and 5-D supercrystals, and figuring out how to actually fabricate this "good ship Synaxis." So that's what I'll be working on this year. Oh, and praying about where the wherewithal is going to come from to build such a vessel: I'm a farmer, not a financier!

Lastly I wish to thank my good sister for not suggesting that the extra wings on the "Christopher" figure in the icon have anything to do with bats in my belfry. And I cannot close without responding to a certain hypothetical scenario about a certain metaphysician flying to the stars, by asking whether the fair astronomer who proposed the scenario would be interested in accompanying him, if he did?

In the meantime let us love one another, as He has first loved us,

In Christ,

Christopher

III.

But the winter of '42 saw our philosopher-farmer occupied as much with practical meteorology as with metaphysical mechanics, and the major increase in snow removal activities made him especially grateful for the small whispers of instruction that still visited him, as he filled in more details of the design. Meanwhile our mathematician and our astronomer-linguist were collaborating directly in the collection of live data, filtered and normalized hypergeometrically, while their spare hours were occupied more with skis than with horses, and some of their not-so-spare hours with preparation for the final examinations for the doctorate. And our theologian, finishing up his second year in Seminary, was immersed in the rich treasury of choric verse and hymnody which furnished the "propers" of the Divine Liturgy, and also in the corresponding mysteries of the liturgical calendar. Again, St. Maximus had much to say on the "divine mystagogy" of traditional Christian worship. In short, a busy winter passed swiftly for our Metaphysicals, and ten days into spring, it was again Maxim who initiated a new cycle of letters.

March 30, 2042 A. D.
Palm Sunday

Dearly Beloved,

Hosanna! Blessed is He who comes in the name of the Lord! Hosanna in the highest!

I greet you on the day of our Lord's triumphal entry into Jerusalem, mounted though He was on a donkey to fulfill the messianic prophecy, just five days before His crucifixion. Great Lent draws to an end, and I am fresh from the Divine Liturgy of St. Basil, with the body and blood of Christ coursing through my veins, as I strive to collect my thoughts regarding the remarkable development, over the past two years, of an emerging sense of a mission involving the four of us. On one hand there is the concentration on Cygnus, from Sophia's reverie on the Swan of the Cross to my vision of a year ago to our ladies' current search for signifying starlight; on the other, there is the astonishing vision which Christopher received on the Eve of last Nativity, essentially providing the structural design of a vessel, but not only that. Remember, in my vision the Christ Child was in the sky, superimposed on the central star of Cygnus—while in Chris's He appeared right there in the barn loft, fifteen feet away! And He spoke! So my soul brother's vision is more than a technical breakthrough: it signifies a spiritual approach from Heaven to Earth, I do believe. I've asked my advisor here about it, and he simply advised that we be careful to discern the Spirit and not to fall for some Satanic delusion. I've also written to Elder Lavrenty, who is back in Russia, by way of Dean Killgower.

I keep coming back to the question of what God has in mind for us, and how it relates to the special harmonic relations of our *logoi* in Christ. Supposing hypothetically that this might involve a voyage to the chief stars of Cygnus in Christopher's good ship *Synaxis*, the question remains, to what purpose? Why would the Lord wish to physically transport four human beings from the final epoch of geocentric time, as much as 1550 LY into deep space? In other words, why outer space at the End of Time? What kind of contribution might this represent to our Eliatic Restoration?

That question being posed, I have a few comments and commendations for y'all. I want to commend the synergy in which Chris and Maria have worked, she following his metaphysical advice on the being of mathematical objects, and he following her hints both geometrical and crystallographic by studies that turned out to furnish integral elements of the spaceship design in the vision, the Lord using the acquired knowledge as a vocabulary for communication. Also I should mention, what our metaphysician knows well enough, that nothing about a drive system or analogous device was included in his report; that is, a technical means of actually moving the beautiful sky-blue sphere across spacetime. I am sure we all look forward to learning more about that.

Of all things, I have an astronomical observation to share, deriving from my sister's report of last September. I find it interesting that both α- and γ-*Cygni*, the top and central stars of the Cross, are about the same distance from Earth and are both moving toward Earth, while Cygnus X-3, from way farther out, is aiming a relativistic matter-energy jet right past γ-*Cygni* on its way straight toward Earth. Just an observation: something to think about.

That's probably enough for this letter. I need to have a good long run before dinner at the home of one of the married priests I mentioned. His wife is charming (though her eyes do not twinkle like someone's I know) and their family life is heartwarming to behold.

I pray steadily for the success of your studies, all three. Beware the evil one.

Hosanna in the Highest!

In Christ,

Maxim

In addition to the usual academic activities involved in finishing out a term—papers, presentations, examinations, etc.—Maxim met several times with the priest in whose parish he would be training over the summer, Saturday through Monday each week. Father Alexander was a kind and sagacious man, for whom Max was happy to be working. Max was also happy to host his blue-eyed mathematician for over a week, right after term like last year, and happier still to feel a slowly solidifying certainty, each time he looked at her, that he was hers. Christopher likewise enjoyed the company of his fair astronomer, who eagerly looked over the technical information he had assembled, including sources and estimated costs for extruded carbon-fiber rods, with connectors bezeled to hold tiny supercrystals, 4-D and 5-D supercrystals themselves, and the technical coated fabrics specified in the vision. Sophie also listened with interest to his speculation regarding a "drive system," in response to her brother's jibe, although every time their eyes met he would lose his train of thought, and end up kissing her to fill the silence. But then she and Maria were off, and the harvest was fast at hand in Pennsylvania. By the first of June our ladies were back in the high Rockies, from which Maria quickly dispatched the following.

June 2, 2042
Feast of the Holy Trinity

Maxim mine ownest, Christopher my brother,
Sophia my linguist of angels,

Glory to the Father and to the Son and to the Holy Spirit, as it was in the beginning, is now, and will be forever! Glory to the eternal and life-giving Trinity, one Essence in three Persons, and to the Second Person uniting that divine Essence with human nature to incarnate as our Lord Jesus Christ! Hallelujah! Amen.

I am doubly inspired to write this letter today, as Sophie and I attended both the Divine Liturgy in the Orthodox chapel, which was glorious, and then Divine Service in the Lutheran chapel, where we chanted responsively the Creed attributed to St. Athanasius, celebrating the amazing symbolic logic of the Holy Trinity and the Incarnation of Christ. Also, since I just talked over most of the following with everyone, I want to go ahead and get it formalized in the letter as we all agreed. So first of all, Sophie and I have taken a cue from Maxim's observation of the grouping of Cygnus α, γ, and X-3 with regard to their distance from, and direction toward Earth, and we have focused on these all spring. By way of reporting our preliminary indication of linguistic form in starlight, let me give you a little primer of our approach. Remember that Sophie defined the elements of grammar as *meaning*, linked to articulate *physical vibration* and subject to *syntactic structure*. It seemed to me intuitively that an array of angelic syntax coded in starlight could be considered geometrically, since spacetime as we observe it is essentially a hypergeometry of light.

The electromagnetic spectrum is conveniently divided into eight "bands," with energy and frequency increasing and wavelength decreasing from radio through microwave, infrared, visible, ultraviolet, x-ray and γ-ray, to cosmic rays like the "cygnets" reported from X-3. Emissions of any single star display variations of intensity (including zero) within each of the eight bands of its spectrum, so I defined a variable duration of time over which to look for correlations between the bands. This amounts to a sort of word (or letter) search. Of course, binary and ternary stars introduce other possible correlations, as does the consideration of any two or three stars as possibly light-correlated. Another complication is that different star-to-Earth distances can introduce substantial time-dislocations in the signals received from different stars: the light from α-Cygni, for example, has roughly twenty-five more light years to travel than that from γ-, so what we are reading from α is about twenty-five years older than what we are reading from γ- at any given time. We actually have enough data from a quarter-century back to look at α- and γ-, but those are the only two close enough together in LYO for this approach. Then too, we must allow that the angels are above time, and so could coordinate the emissions of their associated stars so as to avoid the time-dislocation due to distances.

To make a long story short, I devised a geometrical filter for the spectrometric data that would function as a sort of "syntax detector" using band correlations for words (or phonemes) as described above. We had spent the winter working on the method, so when we turned to α-, γ-, and X-3 this spring we were ready for action. Indeed it is my privilege, dear ones, to formally announce that we do appear to have semantic signals! We have definitely identified a small set of spectral band correlations that display syntactic structure across time, and which are emitted by both α- and γ-*Cygni*. The specific correlations in the light of these two stars, moreover, not only are present in their current starlight, but are readable in the 25-year-old data as well! The main work now is to translate this angelic syntax in terms of its meaning, which we are of course hard at work on even as we continue to watch our stars. Nothing definite on X-3 as yet. I think that both of our dissertation advisors are a little flabbergasted!

And that, my dear fellow Metaphysicals, is about it for now. I would like to add, though, in closing, that I very much enjoyed meeting Father Alexander and his family, and dining with my Maxim in their home, seated blissfully at his side. God bless and keep you all,

In Christ,

Maria

Maxim spent the summer of '42 happily learning the ways of shepherding a parish for three days a week, and just as happily shepherding the flocks of the Lazy M for another three—Friday being his day off. But his thoughts were never far from the awesome developments that had transpired among the four of them since they had graduated Luther-Aquinas: the visions seen by Christopher and himself, and now the discovery by Maria and Sophie of possible communications from the stars of Cygnus, or from their angels. Above all, the question of purpose continued to puzzle him: Whatever could God have in mind? Why outer space, at the End of Time? Christopher, by contrast, was altogether absorbed in the nitty-gritty of a difficult farming season, on top of building a desktop model of the *Synaxis*. The former situation was due to a failure of the weather to cooperate with the farmers, which made for late plantings, to putting more grass into silage than into hay, and cutting some of the low-lying areas by scythe; while the latter challenge involved some tricky calculations (with sisterly assistance) as well as well as patience and manual dexterity in assembling the nested polyhedrons. While their menfolk were thus busied, Maria and Sophia were heavily into their doctoral research, writing up the clear indication of grammatical syntax in geometrically-filtered starlight which they had discovered, while continuing to search for some clue to its meaning. Sophie in particular continued to monitor closely the three main target objects, and also to conduct a quick survey of the remaining three stars of the Cross, namely β-, δ-, and ε-*Cygni*. Then, as September drew near, the heavens declared what they had been waiting for; but we shall allow our astronomer to report her findings to the reader.

September 14, 2042 A.D.
Exaltation of the Holy Cross

Christopher my spaceman, Maxim my brother,
Maria my gentle geometer,

Glory to the Cross of our Lord Jesus Christ. Our
salvation, light and resurrection!

Given the overall drift of this correspondence, now
in its third year, and given the convergence of the
developments recorded here upon the constellation
of the Northern Cross, it has seemed good to me
and to the Holy Spirit to write again on this exalted
festal day. I have a major announcement to make in
this letter, but rather than rush right into it, let me
fill in the background of our summer's work. Maria
reported in June that we had confirmed a "set of
spectral band correlations" in the emissions of α-
and γ-*Cygni*. Further grammatical analysis found
there were six distinct correlations, occurring as two
sets of three, like a two-word phrase or sentence.
Since we still had no real clue as to semantics or
meaning, we turned to the other three stars of
the Cross, namely β- at the bottom and δ- and
ε- on the arms; and since we now knew what to
look for, we quickly found the same grammatical
expression in those spectra as well. In other words,
all five stars of the Northern Cross are emitting the
same message, despite the roughly 1200-year time

lag due to lightspeed between the outer two stars and the inner three. Yet we still couldn't tell what they were saying. So we watched, we prayed, and we waited. Then suddenly, on August 28, the Feast of St. Augustine in the West, everything changed.

Maria and I arrived at the Observatory early, and upon logging onto the astronomical information system were greeted by the news that Cygnus X-3, which had been relatively quiet recently, had loosed a major burst of emissions including a band of cygnet-rays with unusual articulation in time. When Maria ran the whole spectrum through her filters she found the same grammatical form emitted by the five stars, but transposed to higher bands of the spectrum including the cygnets. Then we noticed unusual activity in the radio band, which had not previously been involved in the significant correlations: Each time the grammatical form appeared in the upper bands, a signal with six peaks appeared in radiofrequency. Switching on the audio, we found that as we isolated each of the six peaks in the signal we were able to discern what sounded like a phoneme: first the consonant "y," then a vowel sound, like "ah," then the consonant "l." The second set of three peaks sounded like "k," then a different vowel sound, like "uh," then the consonant "m."

Now you gentlemen have to allow that Maria and

I were a trifle beside ourselves with excitement over what had just transpired, but once we settled down enough to actually put the six phonemes together, the sentence is more or less unmistakable: "Y'all come." Once that sentence had a chance to soak in, all we could do was sit and look at each other with amazement. Anyway, we've spent the past two weeks checking, confirming and writing up this somewhat startling communication, or rather invitation, and it is definitely for real. All that we need now, it would appear, is a vessel to take us safely there, and preferably a clue as to why we are invited to "come"—as the culmination of a whole twenty-eight-month intellectual adventure, including visions of the Christ Child and His angels. In other words my Christopher's spaceship, on which he is laboring diligently, and my brother's persistent question, "why outer space at the End of Time?" As to the latter I haven't a clue. But as to the former, in token of my confidence, I hereby formally (and fondly) apply for the position of staff astronomer on the good ship *Synaxis*, to her commander Christopher Eckhart.

In the excitement of relating our latest findings I have not even mentioned that, just as on the occasions of my two previous letters, I am seated at my big star window on the northern sky, and the Swan of the Cross is beaming its message right onto my forehead as I write, and into my eyes when

I gaze at it. I can almost hear the stars whispering, "Y'all come."

God bless and keep you,

In Christ,

Sophia

By this time, Maxim was into his senior year at Seminary, where he had the solid grounding in homiletical and liturgical practicums—i.e., the art of preaching and the science of worship—to counterbalance the head-spinning news announced by his sister. He had passed along this latest development to Dean Killgower and Elder Lavrenty, but it was hard to keep his mind from dwelling on it, between the demands of his practicums and the thesis he was writing on the *logoi* and *energeia* in St. Maximus compared with the relations of *esse* and *forma* in St. Thomas. Maria and Sophie spent most of the fall term putting their doctoral dissertations into final form, to be submitted by year-end and orally defended in early spring, after review by the relevant faculties. They also continued, of course, to monitor the stars of Cygnus for any further communications that might be forthcoming as new additions to the electromagnetic vocabulary of significant starlight. Christopher, for his part, was enjoying a dry autumn for the late harvests caused by late plantings due to a wet spring, which he considered a fair balancing of accounts on the part of nature, or of the angels who direct her. It was also good weather for cutting firewood, but since there wasn't a lot of sawmill activity this year, he had plenty of time in the *studium*, perfecting the desktop model and pondering, as well as praying over, the problem of the operative means for the ontological teleportation he'd envisioned: the metaphysical "motor" of his *Synaxis*. Then something remarkable occurred, which caused him to write the following letter.

December 25, 2042 A.D.
The Nativity of Our Lord

Sophia my sweet astronomer, Maria my mathematician, Maxim my chaplain,

Christmas greetings, on the day we celebrate the birth in Bethlehem of our Lord and Savior, Jesus Christ, as a little child. I must tell you that the Christ Child is especially on my mind today, for reasons I will shortly explain. But first let me confess that I had reached the brink of despondency over my lack of any breakthrough on how the teleportation could be effected. I prayed hard at the late Divine Service last night, then downed a rare nocturnal cup of coffee and retreated to the study for a long vigil, firing up the stove and settling down with my notebooks.

One line of thought I'd been pursuing begins with Thomas' teaching that every form participates by likeness in the divine act of being, the *esse* of God; so in one way *forma* is in potency to *esse* (since no form actually exists except by participation in the divine *esse*), while in another way *forma* is the principle of *esse* (since in creation God causes natural being by means of form). For example, in beings composed of form and matter, *forma* is the cause of their *esse* by determining the pure potency of their *materia*. Finally every natural being, considered as an agent, always acts in function of its *forma*. But that line of thought always left me feeling as if on the brink of a penetrating insight that always still eluded me. Some sort of formal relation between the geometry of the nested polyhedrons, and the architecture of hypergeometric spacetime, whose curvature equals matter-energy: that was as far as I could get.

Max had been kind enough to share privately a few pages of his work on *logoi/energeia* as compared to *forma/esse*, so I carried out a number of extended cogitations along Maximian lines, with analogous results. I did note, however, that the notion of *participation* was key to the formulations of both St. Thomas and St. Maximus: in the former it was how *forma* receives the uncreated *esse* which it causes to exist as created *esse*, while in the latter it is how the creature, who exists by the immanence of its *logos*, engages the divine *energeia*. Abstractly, I sensed that the breakthrough I sought had to do with a formal participation in *esse*, actual being, perhaps coupled with a *logos*-driven participation in divine energy (as distinct from matter-energy); but concretely I had no idea how to proceed.

Sometime after 2:00 A.M. I decided to read the Christmas sermon of my illustrious namesake, on a text from the book of *Wisdom* which he paraphrased, "For while all things were wrapped in peaceful silence and night was in the midst of its swift course, a secret word leaped down from heaven, out of the royal throne, to me." The sermon in which he says, "I believe more in the Scriptures than I do in myself," and where he says that while we rightly celebrate the human birth in time of the eternal Son of God, "if it does not occur in me, how could it help me?" Referring to the "ground of the soul", which is the intellectual spirit of a human being, the Meister continues, "In that ground is the central silence, the pure peace, and abode of the heavenly birth, the place for this event: the utterance of God's word." As I read slowly through the sermon, I could feel the deep silence of the winter night seeping peacefully into my distended state of mind, calming, relaxing, inducing detachment. In turn I arrived at the sentence: "When all the agents of the soul are withdrawn from action and ideation, then this word is spoken."

As I lingered briefly over this sentence, all at once the voice of the Christ Child, which I recognized from last year, spoke softly but clearly from *within my chest*, "Peace be with you." As I was understandably speechless, the Child continued, "See, I am within you always, as you also are in me. But it is better if I address you from over here," the last sentence indeed sounding to my left, by the workbench on which the model of the ship was standing. As I turned my chair in that direction I saw the Child standing beside the model and pointing to it, with a smile on His face like a kid who just opened a Christmas present. It is no exaggeration to say that His smile was radiant, literally, like everything else about Him—robes, face, halo, and hands—all four feet tall of Him. As He pointed to the model it too began to glow, and falling to my knees before the Child, I gazed in wonder at the nested-polyhedral spheroid which was the fruit of long labor, shining in the glory of the Lord!

The Child interrupted my rapture by saying, "Supercrystals on the model too," and while I was wondering how that made any sense, the whole interior of my study was transformed into a virtual interior of the *Synaxis*, twenty feet in diameter and centered precisely upon the radiant model or miniature. Now the Christ Child, still smiling, gestured toward me, saying, "Rise and walk. Look and see." So I stood up and looked around the spheroid interior of our starship: The level of the deck was three feet below the "equator" of the spheroid, so it was thirteen feet below the apex above, leaving a seven-foot-deep hold below deck for stowage. Around the equator of the spheroid, three feet above deck level, was a continuous desk space, with four revolving chairs at four quarters. Each chair could swivel toward the desk, where a compact information processor with keyboard appeared, and above it a viewscreen in one of the square panels of the inner polyhedron. Or it could swivel toward the model in the center, which stood on a pedestal just tall enough to locate the center of the smaller spheroid in the exact center of the larger one.

I walked slowly around the circular deck, and when I arrived at the side of the model where the Child was standing—the top of His head only inches higher than the apex of the model—He suddenly pointed to the miniature spheroid, still glowing with His light, and said, "Participator," in that magisterial little-boy voice I had come to know, and to love. The model starship responded to being renamed "Participator" by beginning to shine and to pulsate at each of its eighty-four vertices (twenty-four inner and sixty outer), and then to emit visible rays from each vertex to a corresponding vertex in the outer spheroid. Interior coverings grew transparent to reveal the outer vertices linked to corresponding points in the Participator, both sets of vertices shining and pulsating in the vision. Suddenly the rays reverted into the Participator, which glowed a brilliant blue-white and expanded to about twice its diameter, as the Child seated Himself in what had now become the orb of the icon. The flutter of twelve wings announced the arrival of His angelic escort, and "away they all flew, like the down of a thistle." I found myself standing agape in my study, still facing the Participator minus its newly-prescribed supercrystals, which still stood on the oaken workbench in my study.

There! That's the gist of it! So I have some more design and costing work to do, though I still have no operational instructions on actually *using* the Participator, and no answers to the dangling questions of rationale (outer space at the End of Time?) and wherewithal ($$). But this whole thing has developed a step at a time, so we wait for the Lord's next move. And by the way, my sweet astronomer's application for the voyage is happily accepted. Meanwhile, I am going to spend the rest of Christmas (not necessarily all twelve days) eating, drinking, and sleeping! May the ineffable smile of the Christ Child be with you all.

In Christ,

Christopher

As it turned out, our Metaphysicals did not have long to "wait for the Lord's next move". In the meantime, three of them headed back to school for the last time, Maxim to finish the requirements for ordination, including comprehensive examinations written and practical, and the ladies to spend the winter writing articles, giving seminars, and preparing to defend their dissertations. At the same time, Max continued pondering and praying over the "why" of this incredible voyage in the making, while Maria and Sophie kept up their search for additional inter-band correlations of possible grammatical significance. And Christopher the metaphysician found himself working on such mundane matters as negotiating with the crystallography lab he'd located for an additional eighty-four supercrystals of smaller size, designing the deck and the circular desk to be machined and installed by local craftsmen, and firming up quotes on local custom-manufacturing space. In short, they all had their noses to the grindstone when, seemingly out of the blue, the following letter arrived in each of their inboxes.

February 2, 2043
Candlemas

Dearly beloved Metaphysicals,

Grace to you and peace from God our Father and the Lord Jesus Christ.

The four of you have been much on my mind, and on the mind of Elder Lavrenty, especially since Maxim's communication of last spring regarding the visionary developments. Lavrenty and I have stayed in touch since his return to Russia, and the unfolding saga of your spiritual adventure has been a regular topic of our discussion. Then last night, or rather early this morning, I had a dream, which I shall relate to you as clearly as I can recall it.

I am sitting in the Ox & Swan with Elder Lavrenty, at the table beneath the tableau opposite the bar, where you held your valedictory celebration. We are sharing a pint of Augustiner Brau. There is a shout from outside: "Look at this!" Lavrenty and I head outside to see what the commotion is, but on emerging from the tavern we find ourselves, not on the College campus, but standing outside a large industrial building on the outskirts of a small town. As we enter the building by a nearby door, the first thing we see, suspended in a manufacturing bay, is a sky-blue sphere, or rather polyhedron, bearing the name SYNAXIS in white letters. Then we see the four of you approach the vessel, Max clad in a black cassock and carrying a small golden cask and the other three of you in white albs—all four with a blue cincture knotted about the waist—and solemnly enter the blue spheroid, closing the hatch behind you. At this point the polyhedral hull of the vessel grows transparent, so that we can see inside it, as well as audiolucent so we can hear within. We see the four of you seated at quarters around the circumference of the deck, facing a sphere in the center and singing the doxology. When you have sung the Amen, Christopher intones in a strong, clear voice, "*Synaxis*: command mode." To this, what sounds like the voice of a Child replies, "Command mode acknowledged." Then Christopher simply chants, "*Synaxis*: α-*Cygni*." As he is chanting these words, the vessel recovers its original sky-blue opacity, and then approximately one second later, it disappears into thin air. Suddenly we are back outside, and Lavrenty points to Cygnus in the firmament, just as α-*Cygni* at the top of the Cross pulses three times, followed by the exact same pulsation, in turn, of β- at the bottom, δ- on one side, ε- on the other, and finally γ- in the center, which uniquely pulses four times. In other words, the sequence of the stars' pulsations essentially "makes the sign of the cross" on the Northern Cross itself. Then we are back inside the building, and the sky-blue spheroid reappears in the bay where it had been.

That, dear ones, is the gist of the dream. But once I had awakened, prayed Matins, breakfasted, and looked over the collection of candles in the chapel, to be blest as traditional on this day, I checked my messages and found one from Elder Lavrenty. I could not believe my eyes. He reported having dreamed the same dream, about nine hours earlier than I! We quickly compared notes, and the description given above is agreeable to the Elder, with several minor details excepted, which he prefers to mention in person. In fact there are additional details we both would prefer to share face to face. To that end we would like to propose a sort of conventicle in May, based at the College but with perhaps a couple of field trips as appropriate. What do you say, my dear Metaphysicals? Is it a date?

Now I really do have several hundreds of candles to bless, so I (or rather we) shall await your reply with all the patience that the Holy Spirit can supply.

The Lord be with you,

In Christ,

Thomas Killgower

Our four principal protagonists lost no time, via a series of quick back-and-forth communications, in agreeing to accept the invitation of the Dean and the Elder to reconvene at LAEC in late May, almost exactly three years after matriculating there. In the meantime Maxim would complete the requirements of his church for ordination, and consider with his superiors the question of when his ordination to the priesthood should follow, given the possibility of a mission into outer space. In early spring Maria and Sophia successfully defended their dissertations and were awarded their doctorates, respectively, in mathematics and astronomy—actually finding themselves in the news for a week or so when the gist of their discovery was formally announced. Christopher spent the last half of winter negotiating the production of forty-eight 4D supercrystals (in two sizes) and 120 5D supercrystals (in two sizes), by chemical precipitation, within seventy-five days of the date of order; local construction and installation of the interior woodwork, in the same time-frame; delivery of the structural components (rods, bezeled connectors and membranes) forty-five days from the order date; and custom manufacturing space with skilled labor to assist in construction. With the return of spring, the seasonal upturn in farmwork reclaimed his attention, and very soon, so it seemed, May had arrived.

CHAPTER THREE:
THE PENNSYLVANIA
CONVENTICLE

I.

The Reverend Doctor Killgower had made arrangements at the College for a conventicle of three days—a "conventicle" in the sense of having some religious significance and of being slightly secretive in nature. With classes and graduation over, and summer courses not yet underway, the campus would be largely deserted, so the Dean had retained several of the food service crew to prepare meals in the guest cottage. The latter would easily house the five visitors, and was conveniently near the Dean's office and adjoining conference room, where they would conduct their formal discussions. In addition, they could pursue more peripatetic conversations along the College's trails through the surrounding forest, for Luther-Aquinas Evangelical was nestled among the proverbial woods of Penn's Sylvania, in Clearfield county west of DuBois and conveniently close to I-80. As for the dates chosen for this peculiar conventicle, the last three days in May 2043 proved to be Friday through Sunday, wherefore the first entry on the Dean's agenda read, "Friday, May 31, 1:00 PM, Luncheon."

On the morning of that portentous day, Dean Killgower met Elder Lavrenty at the airport, where after exchanging the double kiss of peace, they started off at a brisk pace toward Killgower's car, where they could converse confidentially. Maxim and Sophia had flown in a few days early to visit with the Eckharts, and were riding over to the College that morning with Christopher and Maria, to arrive around noon. As the Dean and the Elder had much to talk over regarding the remarkable events that had brought about this gathering, and what the next several days might hold; so the four Metaphysicals, amid much affectionate holding of hands, produced plenty of palaver on the amazing adventure they found themselves embarked upon, interspersed with fond reminiscences of their college years. By the announced time for the luncheon, all parties were settled in the guest house and assembled around the dining room table, the old men at the two ends and the young men seated on one side, facing their lady loves across the table.

After the food, those who had prepared it, and those who were about to partake of it were properly blest, the Reverend Doctor suggested that their prandial parlance be devoted to light conversation, avoiding matters pertaining to the reason for their assembly until they adjourned to the conference room at 2:00 for formal discussions. For a start he commented on the beauty of the Pennsylvania forest this time of year, and then asked the twins from Texas how their hill country looked right now, and the twins from Clarion county, an hour down the road, how the farm was doing. The ensuing conversation evoked a mental collage of the two geographic regions, similar in that both were on plateaus dissected by streams, but differently adorned as to vegetation, including flowers, and as to birdsong. Glimpses of both nature and agriculture were posed side by side as the voices of the four youths alternated and overlapped, in between bites of the light fare provided for their luncheon and swallows of water and coffee. The creeks were running high in the hill country this spring, which made moving the flocks a little trickier, but the spring flowers were especially flourishing, as were the wild berries, which attracted lots of birds. Clarion County by contrast was a bit dry, making for easy planting but also for reduced growth of the winter wheat and the grassfields, which portended less wheat-straw and first-cutting hay. In such manner, according to the Dean's suggestion, the hour allotted for the luncheon passed amiably, with the four youths chattering away like songbirds, and the two elders listening intently, their old eyes glittering with a quiet gaiety. Perhaps Lavrenty was thinking of spring in the outskirts of Moscow, but in any case he maintained silence.

Upon rising from the table, the party proceeded directly to the Dean's conference room, where a table for twelve allowed them to spread out materials as necessary. As soon as everyone was comfortably seated, their host opened the proceedings.

Rev. Dr. Killgower: It is indeed a delight to see you all again, after a most eventful three years, during which I confess things have not been the same around here without you. And yet my delight is tinged with great solemnity owing to the nature of the aforesaid events, and their culmination, namely the prospect of a voyage into outer space, to certain stars in particular, and according to our duplicate dream, in a more or less definite order. But speaking of the dream, I mentioned in the letter that Lavrenty reported several slight differences in his dream, which he would relate in person, and which I hereby, without further delay, invite him to do.

Elder Lavrenty: First, allow me to extend the greetings, and the blessings, of the abbot of my monastery and of the Patriarch of Moscow, both of whom send you Godspeed in your mission. The first two details by which my dream differed from Thomas's are of the sort that demonstrate our Lord's sense of humor: the glass I shared with him in the tavern was not Augustiner but Russian imperial stout; and the order in which the stars of the Cross indicated your visitation varied in the order of the two side stars, δ- and ε-*Cygni*. That is I saw ε- to the left, flash before δ- to the right, rather than right-to-left as in Thomas' version, just as the Eastern and Western churches make the sign of the Cross in opposite directions. I can imagine our Lord smiling over these details in His artistry—although of course the question of the actual sequence to be followed will have to be addressed. But the other thing I dreamed, which Thomas apparently did not, is that after the four of you entered the vessel, in the very last second before it vanished, I saw the three angels and the seraph, in giant forms of a pale opalescence, surrounding the vessel as they surround the Child in the icon. When the vessel vanished, they vanished with it, as though to accompany it into space. Those are the only differences I can recall between my version of the dream and Thomas' version.

Rev. Dr. Killgower: Thank you, venerable friend, for adding those touches of detail to our dream. For my part, I have recalled two further points which eluded my initial recollections, a rather whimsical one, and a somewhat ominous one. The first is that the factory building in which the starship was docked, had a faint but distinct aroma of roasted peanuts. Is that whimsical, or what? But the other, more somber thing is that, although I did not see the angels accompanying the ship, as did Lavrenty, yet right after the celestial blue orb disappeared, in the instant before we were outside watching the stars, I glimpsed a tall dark shape standing on the far side of where the *Synaxis* had been. The figure was somewhat indistinct, almost invisible in the shadows, but the faint yet persistent impression that haunts me is that it resembled nothing so much as a cross between an angel and a gigantic bat.

Maxim: So that suggests the Adversary is shadowing our mission, even though we've had no apparent interference from the demons during this whole process? Since we've conducted ourselves prayerfully throughout, hopefully we can rule out the possibility that the whole thing is a delusion wrought by Satan, for if we can, the dream simply means that he, or his minions, are keeping an eye on our voyage.

Elder Lavrenty: I commend you for considering the possibility of delusion, but besides your testimony to the prayerfulness of your enterprise, I bring tidings from Moscow to confirm your hope that you are not under delusion. Let me explain. For centuries, there have been hermits in Russia who have cultivated a sort of special devotion to the Northern Cross, not as a natural form of course, but as a kind of icon of the Holy Cross, especially in connection with night vigils. About two years ago, shortly after my return to Russia, several of these hermits began to experience strong impressions of personal revelation while venerating the constellation. The gist of those revelations was that God was about to perform a great work involving the stars of the Northern Cross, something to do with preparation of the "new heavens" which are to be created after the End of Time. Since the impressions were persistent, their venerable recipients reported them to their superiors, who informed the Patriarchate, where the reports were collated and pondered. There was a consensus that the Lord had informed the Church of this matter for a reason, but no idea emerged as to what that reason might be—until I began hearing from Maxim, through Thomas, of what was going on with the four of you. After prolonged and prayerful consideration, it is the judgment of the Patriarchate that your developing mission is indeed the work of the Lord, although we still do not understand His reason.

Sophia: It warms my heart to know that. I too had worried, what if my hypothesis was wrong, and the linguistic modulations in the starlight were not messages from the angels governing the stars, but merely the artifices of demons, delusions by design? So it is truly heart-warming to know the discernment of the Church that our mission is really from God. And yet Holy Church has no more idea than we do, as to "why outer space at the End of Time," in Max's fine phrase?

Elder Lavrenty: No, my dear Sophia, we do not. We have only His hint to the hermits, that it has to do with "preparing the new heavens," and the fact that He appeared to Christopher in His child-form, suggesting perhaps rejuvenation and renewal. As for Thomas' glimpse of the demonic figure after your "takeoff," we also have concerns that, after all, whatever the Lord intends to accomplish with you the Adversary is certain to try to thwart.

Rev. Dr. Killgower: This is most certainly true. We must all remain vigilant. But allow me to add another note of confirmation, this time from the Western church, as to the authenticity of your calling to this mission. I have long been in touch with a network, a kind of "invisible college," of evangelical-catholic individuals with a history of personal revelations from the Lord, especially as related to the discernment of delusions affecting the teaching and practice of the Church. For example, the false teaching that the rapture of the saints will precede the great tribulation has been a target of their unanimous condemnation. Shortly after Christopher's first vision I reported your developments to this group and have kept them informed since that time, which has resulted in several confirming revelations. The latter specifically confirm the authenticity of divine intention driving your mission, and also add one more piece to the puzzle of its nature, namely that it has something to do with Holy Communion. In this connection, Lavrenty and I believe that the golden cask carried by Christopher in our dream contains a consecrated eucharistic host.

Maxim: A consecrated host! Does this mean I'm to be ordained beforehand? My superiors and I have planned to postpone ordination until after the voyage.

Elder Lavrenty: Since you were not in priestly vestments but wore a cassock, your ordination is not necessarily implied. On the other hand, Communion implies distribution, and for that you should at least be ordained as a deacon. In the final analysis, though, this is our Lord's undertaking, and if He wishes you, Maxim, to be ordained one way or the other, He will make it known.

Rev. Dr. Killgower: Well said, venerable friend. We shall return to this question. But here are two of us who've yet to be heard from, and with apologies to Maria, I wonder if our metaphysical spaceman will weigh in to our discussion.

Christopher: With pleasure, sir. And first let me clear up your "whimsical" recollection of a faint aroma of roasted peanuts in the starship factory. It turns out that the building I have located for the assembly, on the outskirts of New Bethlehem, was for years used for manufacturing peanut butter! With that point settled, I need to confess how humbling this whole experience has been for me. After all, I started off with a sort of "great inventor" attitude, full of ideas about metaphysical precursors of physical processes and ontological drive systems, and in the end along comes Jesus and hands me the design for the vessel. Along with that design He has given several hints as to how its structure is related to its capabilities, and even how it operates by verbal command. On top of everything else, He visited me personally in my barn loft, causing me to feel like absolutely nothing in His presence, and then to hear Him speaking from my heart. So the process has been an extremely humbling one, and continues to be so in the course of His ongoing instructions.

Maria: I think I can testify for Sophie as well as myself, so intimate was our collaboration, that we also are exceedingly humbled by the discoveries that the Lord has disclosed to us. Like Chris, we began our search with minds full of theories, theorems, and methods, but it was the visions of our young men, directly from God, that put us on the right track and clarified the mission of which our work is one part. And now it turns out that this mission involves the conveyance of the consecrated body and blood of our Lord to the stars of the Northern Cross, as part of His preparation of the new heavens! I feel completely unworthy to participate in something so momentously holy.

Maxim: But it's the Lord who has chosen us, dearest, in leading us as He has. If He wishes us to carry His sacrament to the stars of Cygnus, and is providing the means for us to do so, hadn't we better take a deep breath, pray hard, and do it?

Elder Lavrenty: That is of course correct, my son, yet the sentiments of humility just expressed are not only appropriate, but crucial to your success. Remember that pride is the first foothold of the Adversary in his assault upon our souls. Consider the humility of our Lord, who has showed Himself to Christopher as a little Child, almost playfully.

Sophia: Yes! Yes! Look at it this way, Maria: It's like we're playing a game with the Christ Child! He has invited us to play this game with Him. It is His game, and part of it is His showing us, little by little, what it's all about!

Christopher: Exactly, my sweetest! And part of that process is the ongoing instruction I have received from the Child's voice, ever since He first spoke to me that Christmas Eve, saying, "Draw what you see in a book, and use it as you are instructed." I became gradually so accustomed to His voice that I could hear it in a whisper when my soul was silent, and even detect its accents in the flow of my thought. Thus He has generously revealed to me numerous details of the design, such as the portable oxygen and water supply, as well as of the operation, such as the ontological shielding that will envelope the vessel when it is activated, and the angelic coupling with the vessel that enables its teleportation. But there are two matters on which this magisterial little boy, who is Lord of heaven and earth, has not informed me: the subject touched on earlier, of the sequence of our visitation to the two lateral stars, and the question of how the construction and outfitting of our good ship *Synaxis* is to be financed.

Sophia: I cannot speak to your second question, O captain mine, but as your staff astronomer allow me to fill in a few details on δ- and ε-*Cygni*. δ-*Cygni* is actually a trinary system about 170 LYO, appearing as one star from Earth but comprising a blue-white giant, a smaller yellow-white star, and a dim orange star orbiting them at a distance. ε-*Cygni*, which appears slightly brighter than δ- but is about a hundred light years closer to Earth, is a single yellow star.

Christopher: Well spoken, fair astronomer. I see two aspects to consider here in comparing the two systems: distance from Earth, and number of stars. As for distance, we will be starting from Albireo (β) at 385 LYO, having come in from our first stop Deneb (α), at 1550. So our third hop, to either δ or ε, will start from 385 and come in closer to Earth, to either 171 LYO (δ) or 72 LYO (ε). Now on the one hand, δ at 171 would be "on our way in" from Albireo, but on the other hand if we hopped all the way in to ε from Albireo, then δ would be "on our way out" to Sadr (γ) at 1523 LYO, which is the central star and our final stop according to the dream. But yet again, since we will not actually transit through the intervening space when we hop from one place to another, the question of one star being more "on our way" than another is a purely intellectual one. As for the number of stars, going from δ to ε would signify three preceding one, while ε to δ would imply one preceding three.

Maxim: As your chaplain, sir, allow me to chime in here. Even though the divine Unity is a Trinity as much as His Trinity is Unity, yet the unity of the Father is prior to the begetting of the Son and the procession of the Holy Spirit. I am not suggesting, however, that we proceed to the unitary system (ε) first, but rather, since we as creatures can only approach the Father through the Son, in the Holy Spirit, my proposal is that we visit the trinary system (δ) first, and then the unitary ε.

Elder Lavrenty: I believe we can settle this matter. Since it was I who dreamed the reverse sequence, ε to δ, and since I can readily interpret the sequence you propose, which runs right to left as I face the constellation, as conforming to the Eastern custom of making the sign, I propose we dismiss this particular variation, unless the Lord somehow tells us otherwise, and settle on the alphabetical order, δ to ε.

Rev. Dr. Killgower: A most gracious proposal, venerable friend, unless *He* tells us otherwise, as you say. So this brings us to Christopher's second concern, namely the matter of the financing. And here the venerable Elder and I bear tidings of just that kind of support, from the Patriarchate of Moscow as well as certain evangelical-catholic philanthropists, who have together pledged the total sum of Christopher's estimate, with reasonable overage as needed. It delights me to see the four of you gaping with astonishment, but yes, your unique spiritual adventure has aroused significant sympathy within the Body of Christ. In the opinion of several of the donors, moreover, our metaphysician has excelled in cost-containment, given the specified high-tech materials, the intricacies of assembly, and the quick delivery times.

Christopher: The economic climate of the Restoration has fostered the development of small local companies specializing in flexibility within a particular type of technology—extruded structural elements, polymer-coated fabrics, industrial crystals. My vendors are happy with the costs quoted, so long as we don't tarry in placing the orders.

And so the afternoon in Dean Killgower's capacious conference room drew to a close amid mutual congratulations and thanks to God, all around, at the seemingly miraculous coalescence of everything necessary for their still-mysterious mission to move forward. The Reverend Doctor suggested they adjourn until 6:00, perhaps stretch their legs about campus or on a forest trail, then reconvene at said hour at the Ox & Swan, which though it was just then closed for business, would be available to them for libations and dinner. Accordingly the two sets of lovers set off briskly onto different trails into the woods, while the two old men ambled slowly about campus, pausing to enjoy the beauty of May in tree and flower. We shall not report their conversations, except to note that they had much to do with digesting the actual prospect of this fantastic voyage, and the imminent necessity of making additional decisions in its regard.

By 6:00 the six were punctually assembled at the legendary tavern, and seated at the table beneath its titular painting at which their valedictory had transpired, and at which the dream of the old men had commenced. On the table stood a large growler each of Augustiner and Russian stout. Maria opened the conversation by asking whether, as staff geometer, she ought to chart the course decided upon, in geocentric spherical coordinates, to which her brother replied that the Child would indeed like to see such a chart, although He is perfectly capable of locating the stars Himself. Sophie, with a smile, alluded again to the Child's playfulness, and then asked what sort of scanning equipment or capabilities the ship possessed, her beloved answering that this too was a purely angelic capability, by which they would be able to access any desired visual contact with the outside of the vessel, in any desired spectral band, as well as relevant data. All this would be accessible by keyboard and display on specified faces of the inner polyhedron. Maxim, his quiet brown eyes turning from one face to another, repeated his puzzlement about the actual meaning, and even some concrete details of this voyage: What would they do at each star-stop? How long would they be gone? It was Christopher who addressed the second question by observing that their ontological state in the activated vessel would be essentially timeless, although they would experience a local flow of time themselves (heartbeat, breathing, body movements). But as far as lapsed time was concerned, since the angels were able to hop from place to place in spacetime, they could arrange to return at the exact same time that they left, or say ten minutes later! But it was Lavrenty who responded to the question of the voyage's meaning, and of the concrete actions to be taken or experienced along its course, by reminding Maxim and others that they had been led step by step throughout the emergence of this God-ordained adventure, learning only as much as they needed to know at each step. This, the Elder believed, was how the entire voyage was likely to unfold, so that the essential point was to take stock of what was required to prepare for the next step.

As the conversation continued, the two growlers were gradually emptied and an elegant dinner was served and dispatched. In seemingly in no time at all the hour was approaching nine, and the Dean quickly summarized the plans they had agreed upon for the following day. They would breakfast at 8:00 and leave for New Bethlehem around 9:00, where they would visit the factory Christopher had chosen for the assembly of the starship *Synaxis*, and meet there the foreman of the assembly team. Then they would drive north to the Eckhart farm for a tour, featuring prominently the barn-loft study where the Christ Child had twice appeared to Christopher, after the noon meal of which mother Eckhart had insisted they partake at the farmhouse. Late in the afternoon they would return to the College for the evening meal and further discussion. With plans for the morrow thus settled, the six went their ways— the Dean to his quarters, the Elder to the cell he had built while resident there, and the young men and women, after a slow perambulation about the campus, to the guest house where Max and Chris shared a double room, and Sophie and Maria another.

II.

"*Come let us rejoice in the Lord, let us shout with jubilation unto God our Savior. Let us come before His countenance with thanksgiving, and with psalms let us shout with jubilation unto Him.*" The expansive foyer of the College guesthouse resonated sonorously with the antiphonal chanting of six voices, as our Metaphysicals and their elderly mentors greeted the second day of their conventicle with morning prayer. "*For the Lord is a great God and a great king over all the earth.*" After chanting several psalms, hearing three texts of Scripture, and closing with the Lord's Prayer, they proceeded to the dining room and breakfasted on cereal, yogurt, toast and eggs, as broadly or as narrowly as desired, not forgetting plenty of coffee. Dean Killgower had arranged to drive the College van for their field trip, so they could all ride together, and shortly after breakfast all hands were duly aboard—the old men up front, Max and Maria in the middle seat, and Chris and Sophie in the back. First they picked up 322 just south of the College and followed it northwesterly toward Brookville, travelling through what seemed like endless walls of greenwood lining the road on both sides. At Brookville they took 28 south, following the Red Bank Creek for a few miles, then picking up Pine Creek most of the way to New Bethlehem, where the road rejoined the Red Bank, on which the town was situated. Along the way, glimpses of red rock strata along the creek banks contrasted sharply with the surrounding late-spring greenery, as the passengers in the van conversed quietly, or watched the scenery sliding past them as they went.

New Bethlehem, Pennsylvania, was originally an agricultural settlement with fruit orchards and other farmlands occupying a fertile valley, and was named in 1756 by a Moravian farmer from the other Bethlehem, further east in the Lehigh valley. The town had also fostered light manufacturing, most notably of fruit preserves and eventually peanut butter, and in the Restoration it had been fruitful with the kind of technical startups mentioned by Christopher, one of which was the company they were visiting today. Entering the town, they passed a row of grand old single-family homes, setting the style for the rest of the residences, all of which were clean and well-kept if somewhat less stately. Arriving at the edge of town, they pulled into the parking area of an aging but impeccably maintained factory building, whereupon the Dean and the

Elder looked at one another significantly. This was indeed the building in their dream.

As they exited the van they were met by a genial man of early middle age, who greeted them affably while introducing himself as the Director of Operations of the firm which had acquired and refurbished the factory. Inviting the six to follow him, he led them through a side door directly into a manufacturing bay, roughly sixty feet square and thirty high, partitioned from the rest of the building by chain-link fencing covered with industrial curtains. Again Killgower and Lavrenty looked at each other, nodding slowly. This was the place alright. The Operations man was pointing out several lift systems and chests of assembly tools, and explaining how his technical crew (assuming that they received the order) would first install 4D supercrystals in the twenty-four bezeled joints that would connect the carbon-fiber rods to form the inner polyhedron, which they would assemble from the top down using lifts, the rhombi-cubo-octahedron being suspended from three anchor points overhead. This would then be covered, panel by panel, with the specified fabric using superadhesive polymers, and fitted with connectors to the outer shell, which would next be constructed around it after its own bezels were fitted with 5D supercrystals, and in turn covered with its own technical membrane, not forgetting of course the entranceway. The visitors asked a number of intelligent questions, to which the affable Director responded with equal acuity, so that at last, after the six had huddled briefly to establish consensus, Christopher was able to make the man's day by informing him that the job was a go, and that he would have a formal purchase order on his desk by the end of business on Monday. On this they all happily shook hands, and bidding the delighted Director a good day, the party piled back into the van for their jaunt to the Eckhart farm.

Following Maria's directions, the Dean took 66 north out of New Bethlehem, then turned off west toward the farm, which lay near the upper reaches of Leatherwood Creek without bordering it. They turned in at a graveled lane and followed it up a slight grade, through fields of wheat on one side and orchard grass on the other, coming to a crest from which the white farmhouse was visible just ahead. To the left and right were more croplands, bordered by trees, and further along the lane behind the house, the great red barn came into view, with a half-dozen outbuildings ranged about it. Pulling in by the farmhouse, they followed Chris and Maria toward the front porch, where they were greeted by the proud but slightly anxious parents of the Eckhart twins, who after all were apparently poised to take off into outer space. The Dean and the Elder were greeted cordially and seated in places of honor directly beside the senior Eckharts, on whose minds lay heavily certain questions regarding this latest undertaking of their offspring.

Mama Eckhart had prepared a large batch of chicken cacciatore containing three chickens, to be served on home-made linguini with fresh-baked bread, and a massive bowl of mixed-green salad from the kitchen garden, garnisherd with pickled vegetables. But once she was seated beside the Reverend Doctor she asked the two young ladies to please serve the food, after the Elder had offered a blessing. In this way, as soon as the "Amen" had been pronounced, she could begin to bring up the questions on which she desired to know the views of these two divines, such as first, was this really God's idea? And second, she wanted to know, was this contraption her Christopher was building really safe? In the third place, didn't the gentlemen think it was time these youngsters settled down, got married, and started having children, instead of flying off into space for God knows what reason? At this point farmer Eckhart placed one hand gently on his wife's and suggested she take some nourishment, since she had worked so hard to prepare it, and since Sophia had placed a generous portion in front of her. This gave the gentlemen in question time to reply, by turns, that it did indeed seem to be "God's idea," according to several trustworthy sources of Church authority, both evangelical-catholic and Russian Orthodox, and that however surprising it might be, the Lord Himself had repeatedly confirmed His involvement, even right there in their own barn! As for the safety of Christopher's "contraption," they reminded her that the design and operation of the vessel, as well as the mission itself, came straight from the Lord, and that a special crew of His holy angels would accompany and protect the spacecraft. And the question of marriage, they honestly believed, would have to be decided by the young men and women themselves, but it was understandable that they would give priority to this mission from God, even though He alone, as she had put it, "knows what reason." Mama Eckhart listened thoughtfully as she took her husband's advice, enjoying her own mama's recipe, and gradually looking more and more at peace.

The Metaphysicals listened intently to the conversation of their elders, exchanging significant glances from time to time, while striving to do justice to the dinner before them, which concluded with slabs of wild black raspberry pie. For this was indeed a noonday farm dinner of which they were partaking, not to be confused with the light fare of a luncheon! As Maria and Sophie rose to collect the plates and utensils, farmer Eckhart proposed a tour of the farmstead to his two distinguished visitors, so the three of them, followed by the two young men, headed outdoors, while the three women cheerfully collaborated in cleanup and conversation. As the five men walked toward the barn, the proprietor pointed out the two equipment sheds off to their left, where the two midsize tractors, hay rake, bailer, and corn picker/combine were housed. To their right, about a hundred feet from the barn, stood two chicken coops connected by a wide, fenced-in yard, where the birds were partly range-fed with chopped grass and beans. Behind and to the left of the chicken coops rose a two-story granary with a broad corn crib on one side, and interior bins for storage of grains and beans for later processing into cattle and chicken feed. And further to the left of the granary, behind the barn, the farmer showed them what he called the "mill," which sheltered both the equipment for roasting and grinding animal feeds, and also the compact sawmill.

The centerpiece of this excellent agricultural arrangement was of course the great red barn, of which the first floor was a "loafing" area for the steers when they were not at pasture, and the second of which had haylofts along both sides. At one end of one of these, elevated on 8x8 posts and accessible by a steep but sturdy set of steps, was Christopher's study. Something like a gleam of paternal pride appeared in the stocky farmer's blue eyes as he turned the tour over to his son.

Entering the study from the door at the top of the steps, the first thing seen by the visitors was Christopher's desk, where he'd been reading when the Child appeared, directly ahead about halfway down the twenty-foot length of the room, and right under one of the windows. The next thing to catch their eyes was the Participator, the sky-blue scale model of the starship that had turned out to figure in its very operation, on a stand in the middle of a long workbench against the opposite wall, also under a window. Had they been able to take their eyes off this fascinating object, they would have seen nearly two whole walls lined with books, namely the walls opposite the desk and the bench. As they closely inspected the azure orb, its polyhedral figure clearly apparent, the metaphysician explained how he intended to install the miniature supercrystals once he had them in hand. He would first remove the outer membrane and disassemble the outer polyhedron, drill tiny bezels into the joints of the inner polyhedron, and mount the 4D supercrystals in all twenty-four joints using industrial high-performance adhesive. Then he would reassemble the outer polyhedron, connected as before with the inner one, drill and fit its sixty joints with miniature 5D supercrystals, and finally replace the outer membrane, resealing the seams with polysulfide sealant and giving the model a fresh coat of celestial blue. Christopher further noted that he had left the notebooks and other drawings in the Dean's conference room, where they had been spread out on the table, but *here* was the concrete result of what he had drawn in a book as instructed by the Christ Child, who had been sitting right *here*, standing right *there*. All five men spontaneously bowed their heads for a moment, then Elder Lavrenty, Dean Killgower, and Maxim each offered a brief word of prayer, after which they descended the steps to the barn floor and walked out of the barn.

As the men headed back toward the farmhouse, the women were seen chatting amiably on the front porch, whereupon they joined company and continued their conversation seated on two porch swings, a deacon bench, and a couple of chairs. It was now mid-afternoon, and presently the Dean observed that, while it would be pleasant to stay longer, he suspected the Eckharts had other things to do before evening, and in any case their party should be getting back to the College, where dinner had been planned as a venue for further discussion, but where a light supper would now be in order in view of the excellent dinner they'd already enjoyed. Mama Eckhart smiled broadly, her dark curls just starting to show some grey, and amid general felicitations and embraces, including the Russian elder sharing the kiss of peace with the Eckhart parents, the Dean shepherded everyone into the van, promising that the young people would be back the following afternoon. Rather than head south to New Bethlehem and return the way they had come, the Reverend Doctor headed north on 66, turned off to the right just past Glade Run, and navigated a series of small but scenic roads through the Pennsylvania forest to intersect 322, which he then took southeast through Brookville and back to the campus of Luther-Aquinas Evangelical College.

The second evening of this curious conventicle commenced promptly at 5:00 Saturday in the sitting room of the guest house, where its convener had furnished growlers and glasses for libations before their suitably scaled-down supper. Sipping his brew, Killgower proposed that their evening discussions be focused upon what questions or issues remained to be solved by way of preparing for the next step in their mission, as Lavrenty had proposed the previous evening.

Christopher: Amen to that, Reverend Doctor. Now it seems to me that the "next step" at this point is to order the materials, assemble the spacecraft, and go visit some stars. So Monday I place the orders and, if my contractors keep their promises, spend the summer overseeing the construction and rebuilding the Participator, mostly evenings and weekends. So what questions do we still have to solve?

Maria: Well, Captain Courageous, there is the little detail of launch date. What is our timeline? Since the holy Child wishes your geometer to chart our course, it would be helpful to know where in space*time* we'll be setting out from.

Maxim: Excellent point, dear heart. And here is another one: The Dean and the Elder dreamed I was carrying a small golden cask as we entered the Synaxis, and that this cask contained a consecrated eucharistic host. But my question is, what do I do with the cask inside the vessel? Am I still holding it? Have I placed it somewhere?

Elder Lavrenty: I cannot recall seeing the cask once you were inside the vessel. What about you, Thomas?.

Rev, Dr. Killgower: No, by heaven, I do not. The cask was clearly in Maxim's hands as he stooped to enter the hatch, but by the time the membranes became transparent and we could see you all, you were already seated, and no, I do not recall seeing the cask in Maxim's hand or lap, or anywhere else in the interior.

Sophia: So that's two questions to be solved. Here's another: What about the vestments? I'm sure we can purchase white albs (should they be hooded?) and Max already has a black cassock. I doubt that sky-blue cinctures are available as such, but we can get white ones and dye them.

Maxim: Good thinking, Sophie. But back to the consecrated host: How and when does it get consecrated? And while we're thinking liturgically, is there more to the rite that we sing before Chris activates the drive than just the Western doxology in your original description?

Maria: Well considered, sweet man of God. And here is one question more: Inside the ship, who Is sitting across from, and next to whom? Did the dream specify a seating arrangement?

Rev. Dr. Killgower: Well, well! It may be a dry spring, but a veritable brainstorm has just washed over us! Let us take stock: We need to determine a launch date; how the consecration of the host will be handled and where it will be stowed onboard; how the vestments will be procured; what exact liturgical rite is to precede the activation of the vessel; and finally what the seating arrangement will be. But having identified the key issues to be solved, let us adjourn to the dining room and talk through these points a bit more thoroughly over supper.

The ensuing discussion, which ran leisurely on until nearly 9:00, determined first that, if the vessel could be ready in just over three months, their target date should be September 14, the Exaltation of the Holy Cross, for reasons that, when considered, seemed obvious. Since Christopher had asked his vendors to quote on short delivery times, as instructed by the voice of the Child, the timing appeared plausible, especially if divine assistance was factored in. Lavrenty in turn proposed that, with the approval of Moscow, he would conduct a Divine Liturgy with Maxim assisting, early on the morning of the launch, to consecrate the host. Regarding the stowage of the golden ciborium in the ship, though, it seemed they were in need of more guidance. As to vestments, Sophie and Maria had decided to cut and sew the albs themselves from fine linen (with hoods at the Elder's suggestion): Sophie would make hers and Christopher's, and Maria would make her own alb and also dye the purchased white cinctures to the celestial blue of the dream. On the topic of the liturgical rite, ending with the Western doxology, which the four of them would celebrate inside the vessel, there was much thoughtful discussion of which the upshot was that, here too, further guidance was needed. When the lingering conversation came round to the question of the seating arrangement, the Dean and the Elder agreed that, after careful reflection, they were quite sure that Christopher and Maxim had been seated opposite each other with the Participator between them, and that Sophia had been seated to Christopher's left with Maria opposite her, to his right. With that matter settled, the only remaining unresolved issues were the location of the golden ciborium with the consecrated host, inside the vessel, and the order of the liturgical rite which was to precede their voyage to the stars. On these two points it was understood that further guidance was needed, and everyone agreed to pray for instruction that night, beginning at the service of Compline with which the Dean had decided to conclude the second day of their conventicle. After the proper psalmody, canticles, and prayers, they sang the Nunc Dimittis, *"Lord, now lettest Thou thy servant depart in peace, according to thy Word ..."*, and bidding one another goodnight, the six headed off to their quarters for sleep, or vigil, as the Spirit moved.

III.

The third day of the Christian conventicle we are chronicling dawned clear and bright, with a refreshing northwest breeze already beginning to dry the campus lawn from the drenching of an overnight frontal storm. The first item on the Dean's schedule was Matins at 8:00 in the outdoor Chapel, to be followed immediately by the Divine Liturgy of St. Tikhon, presided by Elder Lavrenty with Killgower and Maxim assisting. They would then break fast around 10:30, and after taking necessary nourishment (either sparingly or in plenty), would convene in the Dean's conference room for a concluding session.

The four young people met the two old men at the Chapel a little before 8:00, and took their places standing in a row in front of the semicircular seating, facing the great stone altar in the elevated chancel. The Elder walked over and joined them while the Reverend Doctor stood facing them in front of the altar, ready to officiate the service. The early sunshine was already offsetting the slight chill of the morning breeze, and the lingering wetness was unproblematic since they would be standing throughout. From the trees about campus various strains of birdsong wafted into the clear blue sky.

O Lord, open Thou our lips. / And our mouth shall show forth Thy praise.

Glory to the Father, and to the Son, and to the Holy Ghost. /

As it was in the beginning, is now, and ever shall be, world without end. Amen.

Chanting antiphonally in the agreed tone, the Reverend Doctor and the five others opened the Order for Matins, the deep baritone of the former alternating with the varied chorus of the latter as they continued with the psalm canticle and other selections from the Psalter. The four Metaphysicals chanted ecstatically, blending their voices sonorously with the Elder's bass tone and lifting their praise to God amid the sunny breezes of a fine late-spring morning.

The heavens declare the glory of God; / and the firmament showeth His handiwork.

One day telleth another; / and one night certifieth another.

There is neither speech nor language; / but their voices are heard among them.

Praising the glory of their Creator, acknowledging the brilliance of His artistry in creation, they sang His Word with understanding, with realizations and reflections enlightening their hearts (that is, their spiritual intellects), as their voices lifted the psalmody unto the Lord. Now the venerable Elder stepped forward and chanted a lesson from Genesis, the first five verses of that book, evoking God's creation of heaven-and-earth as dark, formless and void, into which by the movement of His Spirit and the power of His Word, He introduced light, and called it Day. To this they responded with the *Te Deum Laudamus* (... *To Thee all Angels cry aloud; the Heavens, and all the Powers therein* ...) and the *Benedictus Es, Domini* (... *Blessed art Thou in the firmament of Heaven: praised and exalted above all forever.* ...), the bright and joyful state of their hearts overflowing into the canonical forms of the Church's prayer. A second lesson was chanted, this time by the Dean, from the second chapter of II Corinthians, where the Apostle argues that since only the Spirit of God comprehends the thoughts of God, and since the Church has received that very Spirit from God, therefore the Church has the mind (*nous*, intellect) of Christ—all this in Killgower's baritone which, if somewhat diminished by age, was yet a serviceable instrument.

Blessed be the Lord God of Israel, / for He hath visited and redeemed His people;

And hath raised up a mighty salvation for us; / in the house of His servant David.

The Matins portion of this morning's worship drew to a close with the foregoing canticle of Zechariah's blessing, the prophecy of John the Baptist's father that Jesus would *"give knowledge of salvation unto His people"* because in Him *"the day-spring from on high hath visited us,"* again sung antiphonally by the Dean and the five. The Apostle's Creed and Lord's Prayer were recited, and with a final prayer, dialogue, and benediction, the rite was concluded. The sun had by now risen higher, shining its welcome warmth upon their bodies as they stood in the cool northwest breeze, under the clear blue sky that arched above the outdoor Chapel.

At this juncture the Elder and the Dean changed places, Lavrenty donning an additional vestment for the Divine Liturgy and standing before the stone altar, while Maxim and the Dean remained standing in a row with the other three.

Priest: *I will go unto the altar of God.*

Response: *Even unto the God of my joy and gladness.*

P: *Our help is in the Name of the Lord.*

R: *Who hath made heaven and earth.*

At the phrase "Name of the Lord," the Elder made the sign of the cross upon the others, who simultaneously crossed themselves in preparation for the penitential phase of the Divine Liturgy. Lavrenty continued:

Almighty God unto whom all hearts are open, all desires known, and from whom no secrets are hid;

Cleanse the thoughts of our hearts by the inspiration of Thy Holy Spirit, that we may perfectly love Thee, and worthily magnify Thy Holy Name; through Christ our Lord. Amen.

A windborne cloud passed across the sun, leaving the Chapel briefly under its shadow and bringing back the chill of the morning breeze, as the state of ecstatic praise to which the Liturgy had lifted their souls yielded to a quiet state of self-examination. Yet this "self-examination" was in reality an examination by God "unto whom all hearts are open"—the all-knowing Lord "from whom no secrets are hid." It was in this awareness that they sang the ninefold *Kyrie* (*Lord have mercy on us. Christ have mercy on us.*). Now, as the obscuring cloud passed on, so the experience of the rite passed on from the painful awareness of sin and shortcoming by the standards of God our Creator to the Gloria, rooted in the song of the angels over Bethlehem.

P*: Glory be to God in high.*

R*: And on earth peace, good will towards men. We praise Thee, we bless Thee, we worship Thee,*

> *We glorify Thee, we give thanks unto Thee for Thy great glory,*
>
> *O Lord God, heavenly King … that takest away the sins of the world …*

This was the Gospel response to the awareness of guilt before

God, the announcement of the nativity of *Jesus Christ ... Lamb of God, Son of the Father*, who became incarnate as the atoning Sacrifice for all sin and guilt, and as the salvation of all who have faith in Him. The remembrance of this Gospel truth washed over the assembled worshipers like a remembrance of each one's Baptism, his or her initiation into the Body of Christ.

The Elder now prayed several short prayers or collects, after which the Reverend Doctor stepped forward to chant the Epistle, from the first chapter of Ephesians, where Paul says that God has "blessed us in Christ with every spiritual blessing in the heavenly places," referring to the spiritual existence of Christian believers *in Christ*, whose sphere of existence encompasses the "heavenly places"; and where the Apostle goes on to say that God "chose us in Him before the foundation of the world," referring to the preexistence *in Christ* of the uncreated ideas or *logoi* of all creatures destined to exist in Him eternally. After the slightest of liturgical punctuations, Maxim stepped forth in turn to chant the Gospel, taken from the sixth chapter of St. John, where Jesus calls Himself "the living bread which came down from heaven," and goes on to promise that "if anyone eats this bread, he will live forever," reminding His worshipers that He had instituted a Sacrament by which they could physically incorporate His risen body into themselves, even as they were in Him, thus strengthening their spirits unto eternal life. And so it was with appetites whetted for the Sacrament that they all recited with sincere reverence the Nicene Creed, sang the Offertory, and harkened intently to Lavrenty's recitation of the Memorial prayers "for the whole state of Christ's Church."

But ere they would receive the bread from heaven and the holy wine, the order of the rite directed them, by the voice of Lavrenty, to "*make your humble confession to Almighty God, devoutly kneeling.*" Moving forward and kneeling on the edge of the elevated chancel, the five intoned:

> *Almighty God, Father of our Lord Jesus Christ, maker of all things, judge of all men;*
>
> *We acknowledge and bewail our manifold sins and wickedness,*
>
> *Which we, from time to time, most grievously have committed ...*

Having earlier been brought to remember in God's sight their sins and failures, now they ask, even plead, that His mercy be applied in judging them, for the sake of His Son, the Lord Jesus Christ. And the Elder, turning away from the altar to face them, invokes the Lord's pardon upon them, accompanied by the sign of the cross, and then recites a series of comforting texts from Scripture for their reassurance. They have arrived at the threshold of the Great Thanksgiving.

> **P**: *The Lord be with you.* **R**: *And with thy spirit.*
>
> **P**: *Lift up your hearts.* **R**: *We lift them to the Lord.*

*P: Let us give thanks unto our Lord God. **R**: It is meet and right so to do.*

This "lifting up of hearts" in the ancient order of worship had long been associated in the Church with the moment when the earthly worship of human beings joins the heavenly worship of the angels, and our four Metaphysicals had early formed the habit of closing their eyes at this point, as they focused their spiritual intellects upon God in Christ, with the hope of sensing the presence of the blessed invisible spirits. The old priest chanted a Preface proper to the day, and then "with Angels and Archangels and all the company of heaven" they bowed their heads for the *Sanctus* (*Holy, Holy, Holy, Lord God of Hosts, heaven and earth are full of Thy glory* …), and then watched and listened with fascination as the Elder consecrated the bread and wine by the very words used by Christ to institute the rite "*in the night in which He was betrayed.*" These earthly "gifts" of bread and wine he then offered to God as fulfilling the command to "*do this in remembrance of me,*" and then called down the Holy Spirit upon this bread and wine so that it be made the Body and Blood of Christ.

> *Grant that we, receiving them according to Thy Son our Savior Jesus Christ's holy institution,*
>
> *in remembrance of His death and passion, may be partakers*
>
> *of this most blessed Body and Blood.*

Next he offered the very participants of the Liturgy, "*our selves, our souls, our bodies*" as a "*reasonable, holy, and living sacrifice.*" They prayed the Lord's Prayer, after which Lavrenty broke the small loaf of bread with the appropriate prayer, and exchanged the kiss of peace with everyone. They sang the Lamb of God (*Agnus Dei*), and after a few other liturgical proprieties had been carefully observed, they each received a large chunk of the bread of heaven, and a moment later a good swallow of sweet red wine which mystically was also the Blood of Christ. The combined effect of well-masticated wheat bread and a swallow of strong wine upon worshipers who'd been fasting for some fifteen hours, lent a heartfelt vivacity to their final Prayer of Thanksgiving *(... and that we are very members incorporate in the mystical body of Thy Son ...)*; and found them, after Lavrenty's invitation to "depart in peace," feeling truly blessed by his final blessing and by the Prologue of St. John's gospel which he chanted as a sort of postlude.

> *In the beginning was the Word, and the Word was with God, and the Word was God. The same was in the beginning with God. All things were made by Him; and without Him was not anything made that was made. In Him was life, and the life was the light of men.*

The mid-morning sunshine now fell brightly upon the tall Elder, clad in priestly vestment, and upon the five devout worshipers who faced him as he intoned the sacred text.

And the Word was made flesh, and dwelt among us, and we beheld His glory, the glory as of the only-begotten of the Father, full of grace and truth.

On the words, "And the Word was made flesh, and dwelt among us," the five bowed deeply, and at the reading's conclusion they responded, "Thanks be to God." Lavrenty walked forward and shook hands with everyone, then slipping out of his vestment he joined them in following Dean Killgower to the guesthouse for brunch.

The latter repast was more than ample for the needs of six adults, four of them young, to break a fifteen-hour fast, but the minds of all, being still infused with the mysteries in which they had just partaken, were perhaps more on those mysteries than upon the meal before them. This inward preoccupation, however, did not serve to divide them from one another, but to unite, since that with which they were preoccupied was one and the same. Gradually, this profound inward unity gave voice to several strains of light conversation—the beauty of the morning, and of the Divine Liturgy under the blue sky, the excellence of the breakfast the Dean had arranged, the loveliness of the two young ladies, and so on. But by well before 11:30 the Reverend Doctor had shepherded the group across the campus to his office, striding amid the greenwood and the birdsong, and assembled them once again in his conference room.

Immediately there was a muffled exclamation from Christopher, who had noticed at once that the notebooks and materials he'd left there on the table were not in the order in which he had left them. This initiated a brief discussion of who might have moved them for some reason, which ended when Lavrenty observed that agents of the Adversary were everywhere, and may have done a little spying, as they were certain to be interested in this affair. With that sobering possibility in mind, Killgower proposed to the group a simple agenda for this final session of their conventicle: First they would resolve the two issues remaining from the previous evening's session; and then they would go over the things to be done in the three-and-a-half months remaining until the agreed launch date. As for the first two issues, the Dean continued, he and Lavrenty had again dreamed an identical dream, which resolved both issues at a stroke, and with the taciturn Russian's assent he went on to explain.

This time the dream had begun just as the Metaphysicals were approaching the ship, and the double hull of the vessel had immediately turned transparent, so they had clearly seen Maxim enter last, inserting the golden cask into the replica hatch of the Participator almost up to his elbow, before taking his station like the rest of the crew. Then, it was he who had led the activation rite, beginning with the *Gloria Patri*, chanted; then Psalm 148, antiphonally; followed by the opening dialogue of the Great Thanksgiving, after which Maxim led them in the Doxology heard by the old men in their original dream. A simple, four-part order. Then the dream had ended.

This rather stunning news, not surprisingly, was greeted with cries of acclamation, quiet and not so quiet, at the Lord having once again given them just what they needed, just when they needed to have it revealed. Christopher was prompted to observe that given the length of Max's arm it seemed the golden cask ought to occupy the very center of the Participator, and that he would therefore plan to include a central housing (or monstrance) in the core of the miniature when he rebuilt it, as well as designing and ordering a small cylindrical ciborium to fit. In addition he would place all purchase orders the following day, Monday, and would oversee the assembly of the starship in New Bethlehem. Maria piped in that, for her part, she would get to work charting their course to the stars of Cygnus and back according to the wishes of the Child with whom they were playing this amazing game. She would also be sewing her alb and dying the specified cinctures of celestial blue, the white originals of which she was quite sure her mother could locate through a committee at church.

Maxim's primary assignment was spiritual preparation, Orthodox and Evangelical, for his chaplaincy on the mission, in close consultation with his superiors in Texas and with Lavrenty and Killgower. Sophia's task, in turn, was to design the system of desired sensor functions and display formats which the crew of angels would use to adapt their intellectual powers to the sensory needs of their human crewmates. She also had two albs to sew, one for herself and one for her Christopher, whose measurements, she confessed with a blush, she was looking forward to taking. The Reverend Doctor announced that he had been appointed executor of the funds collected in support of the mission, and that he had established an account with a local bank, from which any and all invoices submitted by Christopher's vendors and contractors could be promptly paid. Meanwhile he would be in close contact with the "invisible college" of prophets he had mentioned, and with Elder Lavrenty in Moscow, regarding any new signs that might need to be communicated to the four principals, as they each made preparation for the voyage. Lavrenty himself, as just implied, would return to Russia until shortly before the launch, when he would come back to Pennsylvania to participate in the final preparations.

With the Dean's agenda thus largely completed, the matter of Christopher's disarranged notebooks and the possible involvement of Satan was mentioned again, this time in connection with Killgower's dream of a demonic entity present at the launch of the starship *Synaxis*. In the opinion of Lavrenty, since this undertaking was clearly sponsored by the Lord, and since a cadre of His holy angels had evidently been assigned to the mission, it was doubtful that the enemy could accomplish any real disruption. However, it was imperative—and here everyone nodded in assent—that they each pray constantly for support and protection as they worked through their assignments over the summer, and that they be vigilant for any additional signs of demonic interference. They could be sure that the prayers of many others, Orthodox and Evangelical, would accompany them.

On this note the final session ended, and with it the unusual conventicle convened on this weekend in green Pennsylvania, the Dean admitting that Mama Eckhart had confided in him that she would hold Sunday dinner for the four young folks until they were free. And since he would be driving Lavrenty to the airport in the afternoon, and they had wonderfully concluded their affairs, the Metaphysicals were indeed free, and Godspeed.

CHAPTER FOUR:
VOYAGE TO THE STARS

I.

The summer of 2043 passed swiftly for our Metaphysicals. The two young women had obtained ten-week fellowships at Creation A&M, where each would do some teaching while Maria worked out the hypergeometry of the trip, and Sophia designed the sensor and display schematics in addition to keeping their five stars under close observation. Maxim's diocese had ordained him as a deacon and assigned him to a local parish for the summer, allowing him again to lend a hand riding the herds of the Lucky M for several days a week. And Christopher, having indeed placed all purchase orders for the construction of the vessel during the first week of June, had divided his days between the farm and the old peanut butter factory in New Bethlehem. Since Labor Day fell on September 7 that year, exactly one week before the launch date, the four had decided to reassemble at the Eckhart farm by Tuesday the 8th; that is, the other three would join Christopher there, giving them several days of delighted reacquaintance and last-minute preparations before the arrival of Killgower and Lavrenty on the weekend. The picture of their summer that emerged through numerous conversations over those several days was roughly as follows.

Maxim had devoted much of his study over the summer to the subject of angelology, given that his initial vision of Cygnus had portrayed a *synaxis* or communion of angels associated with its stars, and that they would evidently be traveling in the company of, and indeed by the power or energy of, an angelic crew. His studies had led him to Augustine and to Aquinas, who seemingly had more to say on the subject of the angels than his beloved Maximus. Metaphysically, he had learned, the angels could be described as incorporeal substances, real things without bodies, and as purely spiritual beings residing ontologically in the spiritual order of creation without psychical or corporeal components. An angel could also be considered as a composite of *intellectus* and *esse*, the spiritual power of understanding, and the being received from God which caused him to exist; furthermore, each angel was endowed by God with a specific set of innate ideas, making him a species unto himself. In addition, the ideas of all created things, corporeal and spiritual, could be understood to be impressed as images upon the angelic mind of every one of these spiritual creatures, as well as the natural ideas specific to himself. Since the spiritual order of creation is metaphysically above spacetime, the angels do not naturally exist in spacetime, but they can operate there by occupying *intensively* the place occupied *extensively* by whatever body of matter-energy they act upon.

Maxim had been particularly moved by Augustine's emphasis on angelic worship, the angels' worship of God, especially the participation of the angels in human worship that enabled human participation in the angelic worship of the Holy Trinity. Still more significant, he thought, was the role Augustine assigned to this coordinated worship in the spiritual warfare against Satan, since the essence of the Adversary's tactic is to lure the soul into putting the self before God (thus substituting a cult of the ego for true worship), and since the angelic worship of God provides both an example and a support for the human soul under spiritual attack. And speaking of spiritual attack, Maxim had admitted to the others that, of all things, he had been troubled by lust this summer, as his diaconal duties put him in touch with several attractive young ladies with somewhat eloquent eyes, one of whom had asked him for a date. While he had been outwardly the very picture of diaconal comportment, the demons had flooded him with fantasies which he would be ashamed to describe, although God knew them, and it was by turning to God in daily worship, side by side with angels as he now believed, that he had resisted the embarrassing desires until they had subsided.

For her part Maria had been quick to reply to the latter part of Maxim's news, that if she ever were able, God willing, to get her brave theologian down the aisle and to become his wife, she would be happy to show him what to do with his lust. Her own primary temptation this summer, she confessed, had nothing to do with young men, but rather with the most basic sin of all, virtually the root of all sin, namely pride. Even though Lavrenty had clearly warned them back in the spring to beware of pride, it had been all she could do stop patting herself on the back whenever she reflected on the groundbreaking geometrical methodology she was developing to chart the course of their voyage in geocentric spacetime coordinates. Then too, as the demons never failed to remind her, it had been she who had developed the geometrical filter that had enabled Sophie's linguistic analysis of starlight. But she too had fought the good fight, always enabled by the Holy Spirit to recognize the uprising of pride and to dismiss it as the demonic delusion it was, designed to distract her from the work at hand, which the Christ Child had assigned her. And the assignment had been no simple one.

To begin with, there were two questions to be answered, both involving the time-dimension of the course to be charted in spacetime: at what time coordinate they were to arrive at each star, and at what time, how long after takeoff, were they to arrive back in New Bethlehem? A couple of consultations with her brother, who was the one receiving instructions from the Child, had sufficed to answer these: they were to arrive at each star just as it was emitting the light that would arrive at Earth at the moment of their return, which was to be set for ten minutes after takeoff. In other words, they were to return to Earth at the same time as the starlight that left the five stars at the times of their respective visitations, returning shortly *after* takeoff so as not to form a closed loop in spacetime. This had presented some fascinating geometrical problems to our blond geometer, which had required her to prove several new theorems involving 4-dimensional spherical coordinates. These enabled her first to locate each star on a radial vector originating in the launch bay at New Bethlehem, then to calculate the three angular coordinates "locking in" the specified spacetime location, five light-minutes from each star at the designated "Earth-date." In this geometrical frame she had then been able to plot their "hops" from star to star, and back home, employing her new theorems to good effect. Her fellow Metaphysicals all agreed it was easy to see how she could've been tempted by pride, their congratulations putting a twinkle in her bright blue eyes.

Sophia was particularly touched by her friend's confession, as her own stumbling block this summer had been, she bashfully admitted, none other than *envy*, specifically envy of the very accomplishments that had tempted Maria with pride. After all, she had hardly been unaware that her linguistic discovery was dependent on Maria's geometrical method, and when she'd compared her roommate's current achievements to her own relatively pedestrian assignment, the feelings of envy had set in. As she was struggling with these feelings, prayerfully striving to keep them in the perspective not only of her deep friendship with Maria but of their spiritual bond in Christ, a message arrived from her "beloved captain," conveying further instruction and encouragement from the Child Himself in addition to warm personal assurances of confidence and affection from Christopher. This news had put her back on an even keel, and she agreed with Maria that the envy she had felt was doubtless a demonic distraction from her assigned work, the design of the sensor and display modules to be operated by the crew of angels.

Since the *Synaxis* had no windows, and would be ontologically insulated from the physical spacetime surrounding it, the angels would be tasked with sensing metaphysically the ambient array of radiation, and converting it intellectually into optical images or relevant data for display as specified. Since the Archimedean polyhedron forming the inner hull of the vessel had four large squares, separated by triangles, around the slant ceiling above the deck, and a fifth square directly overhead, these five squares had been designated for optical display. Desired tabulations of data could also be displayed on any of the squares, or on the screens of the terabyte notebooks with which each of the four would be equipped. For example, any or all of the five virtual screens could be configured to function as windows, projecting the actual view to be seen if the squares had been transparent to the outside. Any of these views could also be rendered telescopically, either as a zoom-in on a nearby object or as a zoom-out into deep space, and any of them could be displayed across the whole spectrum of electromagnetic radiation, from radio-wave to gamma-ray. Sophie had written all this up, schematized with technical precision, and had placed the documentation before the small icon of the Synaxis of Angels which she and Maria had set up, as instructed by the Child through Christopher. So that ball was now in the court of the angels, as it were.

Our astronomer bore news of quite recent communications from their stars, as well: The reader will recall that the original communication from the stars of Cygnus, consisting of a simple invitation expressed in American vernacular English, had been detected from all five stars simultaneously, as well as from the X-3 source. This time, our astronomer reported, the stars or rather their angels had "spoken" in turn, one word apiece, in the very order in which they were to be visited, $\alpha > \beta > \delta > \epsilon$, after which Sadr ($\gamma$), the last on their itinerary, had emitted a four-word string. Now the first four words, emitted one by one, had formed the imperative, "Lift up your hearts", the opening line of the Great Thanksgiving in the Liturgy, to which the communicants respond, "We lift them to the Lord." The four words spoken by Sadr, then, had continued the liturgical dialogue, "Let us give thanks" being the first four words of the next line, leaving "to the Lord our God" as an ellipsis. The angels were playing the priestly role relative to the Earthlings! But more on this later.

Christopher reported the most "interesting" summer of his life, divided as it had been between the usual agricultural routines of summer, the reconstruction of the model starship as a "Participator," a key component of the "drive" system, and the supervision of the construction of the starship itself, down the road in New Bethlehem.

The second of these activities included the fabrication of a receptacle for the golden ciborium, in the very center of the miniature starship and accessible by its entrance hatch, as well as designing the small cylinder itself and having it cast by a goldsmith. It also included the installation of 4D supercrystals in the vertices of the inner polyhedron and 5D supercrystals in the vertices of the outer polyhedron, materials which had not materialized exactly according to the schedule he'd laid out, due to an unfortunate explosion in the crystallography lab where they were being produced. This of course had impacted the starship construction as well, and although the supercrystals were delivered before the drop-dead date, their lateness had disrupted the planned assembly sequence, which triggered further problems requiring seat-of-the-pants management. The long and the short of it was that the final touches were being finished up this very week before the launch, and the final QC inspection would not be done until the very morning of September 14, even though the crew had worked a half-shift on Labor Day. For his part, he was just thankful to God that the farm had run smoothly this summer.

Christopher's summer temptation had been a burning anger, sparked not only by the supercrystal debacle and its consequences, but by the dozens of more or less minor setbacks and annoyances that had accompanied the entire project. This was on top of the anger that was natural to a man who worked the soil (he had meditated long over this), the very soil that bore the curse of the Creator because of the sin of the first humans, and which never failed to exact its tithe of blood, sweat, and tears from the toil of the farmer, despite the benefits and blessings of that vocation. This burning anger, moreover, had occasionally flared to the point of infecting his vocabulary in ways that could not possibly pass theological or catechetical muster, specifically with regard to the second commandment. Like the others, he'd struggled manfully with this offense, the use of God's name to express anger at created things and situations resulting from the fallen state of earthly life, instead of using it properly for praising and thanking God for making His creation good and beautiful, and for promising to make it new in the End. After consultation with his chaplain in Texas, he had added a short period of afternoon prayer to his daily routine, along with morning prayer in the farmhouse and compline before falling asleep. This change was made in view of Augustine's point about the central role of worship in spiritual warfare.

Such is the gist of the picture that was painted over many conversations among the four, during the week before launch. On Saturday afternoon they were joined at the farm by Dean Killgower and Elder Lavrenty, who had accepted the offer of the Eckharts to board there for the weekend. The six immediately headed for Christopher's study, promising to be ready for supper promptly at 6:00, and talked for several hours about their state of pre-paredness for the climactic event that was scheduled to take place in just over forty-eight hours. Each of the old men had additional tidings to impart, beginning with Killgower's word from his "invisible college" of evangelical-catholic prophets concerning a further incremental insight into the meaning of the imminent mission. The reader will recall that this group had earlier asserted a connection with Holy Communion, from which the inclusion of a consecrated host had been inferred. This time, their insight implied that the sequential visits to the first four stars $(\alpha, \beta, \delta, \varepsilon)$ were to prepare the voyagers spiritually for a culminating experience at the fifth (γ), in which the Holy Communion would actually be involved. In the latter connection, Lavrenty bore a message from Moscow of a theological nature, besides a couple of more practical points, affirming that the eucharistic Sacrament embodies the incarnate Christ, firstborn of the new creation. Therefore the real presence of Christ in the consecrated host anticipates ontologically the final regeneration of all creation, the new heaven and the new earth, a theme which the hermits of Moscow had previously connected with the purpose of the mission. These hermits had also relayed a final vestamentary instruction, namely that the four should be shod in "fisherman sandals" of pure leather, four well-fitting pairs of which, made, blessed and prayed over at the hermitage, were sent along with the instruction.

The other point addressed by Lavrenty was a strong confirmation that the Adversary was indeed aware of their mission and, predictably, was inimical to its success. Not only had this discernment been confirmed by the Russian hermits, the Elder pointed out, but their own experiences of excessive temptation over the summer, including the explosion in the supercrystal lab, certainly suggested a plan of opposition for whose further efforts they must remain vigilant. Dean Killgower strongly seconded this cautionary note, adding that he had himself noticed a certain darkening of the spiritual climate of late, a perception confirmed by his invisible college, portending perhaps the first waning of the Eliatic energies of the Restoration, or even the beginning of the final ascendancy of the forces of the Antichrist. To this somber observation the Reverend Doctor added his own confession of having been sorely tempted this summer by *doubt*, not of the essential doctrines of the faith but of the divine inspiration of the mission. Even as the components were being manufactured and the ship assembled, and the Metaphysicals were carrying out their assignments in preparation, their dear old mentor had been worried about whether Christ would really appear as a Child, or whether what Christopher saw was an image generated by an angel—and if an angel, what *kind* of angel? After prayerful consultation with his network and with Lavrenty, his worries had been resolved by the consideration that surely Christ *could* appear to a man in His incarnate body as it had appeared at the age of six or seven. And if Christ *had* sent an angel in His stead, to produce His appearance as a Child, both the image and the voice would still be the very image and voice of Christ, just as the reality of a sacred Person abides in an icon.

Their conversation being abruptly interrupted by the ringing of the dinner bell, the four young people and the two old men made their way down the steps from Christopher's loft study, and over to the farmhouse for supper. Lingering over Mama Eckhart's country cuisine and abundant beer from the farmhouse cellar, the eight of them refined their plans for the final two days before launch. On the next morning, Sunday, Lavrenty would celebrate Divine Liturgy in the living room of the farmhouse, which could readily accommodate the present company with a little rearranging of furniture, the elder Eckharts having agreed to stay home from church in order to participate. After the noon meal they would all drive down to New Bethlehem and have a close look at the starship, inside and out, now that it was ready to go except for a final quality-assurance inspection on Monday morning. Sunday evening they would again congregate in the farmhouse for prolonged conversation, beginning with an unusually large evening meal due to the fact that the Metaphysicals would be fasting on Monday prior to their 7:00 P.M. launch. This prescribed fast was not only for spiritual reasons but also for metabolic ones, since the ontological state in which they would be subsisting inside the activated starship would be metaphysically detached from the surrounding physical spacetime. Therefore, their natural metabolic processes would be transposed into a dynamic stasis employing only oxygen and water, and sustaining their bodies until their return to Earth just ten minutes after takeoff, in local time.

It was a bright Sunday morning, and broad beams of late-summer sunshine flooded the living room as Lavrenty and the others took their places for the Western Rite of St. Tikhon, with Maxim assisting the Elder and the Reverend Doctor to chant the epistle lesson. Having already attempted, in the previous chapter, to evoke significant glimpses of this sacred Rite, we leave the effort to the reader's imagination, except to note that the voices of the elder Eckharts lent wonderful breadth to the worshipful chanting. After the service they enjoyed a fairly light midday meal, the main repast for the day being reserved for evening for the reason already mentioned. Then they drove down to New Bethlehem in the Dean's official van, a bit crowded but congenial, and disembarked in the parking area outside the starship factory—or should we say the spaceport? Christopher opened the double-locked entrance door to the manufacturing bay, using a mechanical key and a combination code, turned on the lights inside, and beckoned the others to enter.

The assembly crew had set up small banks of LED floodlights in each corner of the bay, focused with breathtaking effect on the celestial blue polyhedral starship suspended from above, with its lower extremity resting on the floor. The cerulean spheroid virtually gleamed like a celestial body itself as the exhilarated crew and their elders walked slowly around this unlikely starship, finally gathering in front of a rectangular opening in one of the large pentagons of the outer polyhedron. With Christopher in the lead, they stooped slightly to enter the hatch, ascended a steep flight of steps, and emerged on the pine deck about six feet from where the Participator was mounted on a sturdy pedestal, in the exact center of the ship. The deck-level cross-section of the inner polyhedron was octahedral, and its walls were furnished with continuous protruding desk space broken only by the entrance way, with swivel-seats for the crew at opposite vertices of the octagon. The interior was entirely painted a bright bluish-white, including the wooden pedestal on which the Participator stood, while overhead the five large square panels, which would function as display screens for the angelic sensors, were clearly visible as outlined by the inner structural elements of the hull. Dimmable LED lights were installed at the corners of the square overhead, providing ample illumination to the concave space in which our Metaphysicals would subsist during their mission. There was also a terabyte notebook, compact but with keyboard and screen of convenient size, on the desk space by each of the crew stations, and Sophie explained that these could be used to access specific images or other data from the angelic crew, according to code she had written.

Christopher pointed out that a large state-of-the-art battery mounted in the hold below deck was designed to suffice for lighting, electronics and atmospheric control, and if necessary it could be recharged photovoltaically by the angels. Also stored below deck were tanks of water and compressed oxygen, and a simple system to maintain exact levels of both in the ship, which would be all they would require in the transposed metabolic state. After everyone had carefully examined everything, and admired the craftsmanship of the local carpenters who had done the woodwork, they backed down the stairs, exited the starship, and again gazed with wonder at her sky-blue hull gleaming in the floodlights. Christopher noted that before activation he would personally place the two hatch panels over the entrance through the two polyhedrons and activate the magnetic seals, this being his responsibility as captain. And exercising the same responsibility, it was he who secured the double lock on the door of the bay, as they left the building and piled back into the Reverend Doctor's van for the ride back to the farm.

Over the substantial Sunday evening supper prepared by Mama Eckhart and the young ladies, conversation turned to the extraordinary liturgical communications received from the five star-angels who had originally invited them to visit. In the new transmissions received by Sophie barely a week before, the governing angels of the five stars on their itinerary had jointly assumed the priestly role in the dialogue that initiates the eucharistic portion of the Liturgy. After the Great Thanksgiving, the reader will recall, the Rite proceeds through proper prayers and the Words of Institution, to the consecration and distribution of the bread and wine as body and blood. Since the voyage was expected to culminate in a eucharistic action, it appeared that the angels had already initiated the Liturgy which would encompass its still-mysterious course. A sense of great reverence descended upon the table as they pondered this remarkable realization, and it was decided on the spot that the four would chant the Great Thanksgiving before entering the vessel on the morrow. After a leisurely meal, they passed another hour or so in conversation, seated on the front porch or ambling about the farmstead, until the satisfactions of a full day had prepared them for sleep, and then they slept in God's peace, and awoke refreshed.

Monday, September 14, 2043, the Exaltation of the Holy Cross, dawned clear and cool in western Pennsylvania. Since the manufacturing team were conducting their final quality-assurance inspection of *Synaxis* in the morning, the Metaphysicals and their mentors had decided to drive down to the ship about noon, which would give them the morning to spend with the elder Eckharts at the farm, and still allow plenty of time for spiritual preparation in the launch bay before takeoff at 7:00 P.M. Accordingly they met the operations director there shortly after noon, where Christopher reviewed the QA documents and signed off on the final payment; the smiling manufacturer departed, wishing them safe travels.

The hour of the launch, just minutes after sunset, had been set by the Child, and gave them all afternoon to get the feel of the ship and to prepare spiritually, as best they could, to meet "face-to-face" the angels who'd invited them to the stars. The Dean and the Elder both prayed over them, laying their old hands on the four young heads, after which Lavrenty systematically censed the whole area of the bay, corners included, with frankincense and myrrh, while he and Killgower chanted formulas of exorcism from the baptismal rite. As they circled closer to the ship, clouds of fragrant smoke rose along the polyhedral hull while the old men sang psalms of blessing and protection. Meanwhile the Metaphysicals had assembled inside, seated at their stations, where they prayed by turns that their voyage would be to the glory of God, and would fulfill the mission on which He was leading them. Then Maxim reviewed the activation rite which would summon the angels, and Christopher reminded them of the subsequent procedure by which he would instruct the angelic crew to insulate and relocate the ship, initially to α-*Cygni* or Deneb, which would also activate the sensor system. Sophie observed that it would of course be impossible to test the latter prior to activation, but she was able to walk them through the menus on their individual notebooks, by which they could access views and data not displayed on the large overhead screens. These latter displays would be controlled by the captain, with counsel from his brown-eyed astronomer. Also available on the notebooks was Maria's hyperdimensional cartography of the voyage, of which she cheerfully showed them the ins and outs.

Although they had bathed and put on clean clothing at the farmhouse before driving down, they had decided not to don their vestments until shortly before entering the ship for launch. But the seemingly long afternoon passed swiftly, almost, as one of them remarked, as if they were already outside of time, and at 6:00 they began taking turns by gender, behind a curtain in one corner which served as a makeshift sacristy, changing into the prescribed ritual garments for their high adventure. The time remaining before they would board the Synaxis at quarter to seven, was passed in processing slowly around the ship, singing hymns, psalms, and spiritual canticles, until Lavrenty and

Maxim stopped in front of the entrance hatch, the others gathering around. Lavrenty solemnly handed Maxim the golden ciborium containing the entincted host which had been consecrated at Divine Liturgy the morning before, then retired with the Dean toward the door of the bay, leaving the four Metaphysicals standing in front of the hatch.

The solemn beauty of the scene is worth picturing: In the background hovered the celestial blue polyhedron gleaming in the lights, twenty feet high by twenty feet wide. In front of the ship, with his back to the open hatch, Maxim with his full dark beard and black cassock towered over the other three in their white albs, with Christopher's sandy hair to be seen but both young women hooded. Each of the four was girded with a bright blue cincture matching the hue of the starship. The following dialogue ensues between Maxim and the three:

The Lord be with you. / And with your spirit.

Lift up your hearts. / We lift them to the Lord

Let us give thanks to the Lord our God. / It is right to give Him thanks and praise.

Stepping to one side, Maxim bowed slightly as Maria and Sophia proceeded past him to the entrance hatch, stooping a bit as they entered and hitching up their albs for the steep ascent to deck level. Now the tall chaplain turned and followed them, stooping deeply, and stepping adroitly under the hem of his cassock he cradled the small ciborium carefully as he climbed. Christopher in turn, with a gallant wave to the waiting old men, entered the hatch and secured the sky-blue entrance panel behind him.

The Reverend Doctor Killgower pulled out his watch, which had been carefully synchronized with the ship's clock. The voyagers had been inside the ship long enough to have taken their stations and to have celebrated the activation rite. The watch said 6:59:50, and he started to count down in a whisper, 9, 8, 7, 6 .... He returned his spellbound gaze to the gleaming blue polyhedron which, just then, vanished from sight.

"Did you see them?" Lavrenty asked him. "Did I see whom?" he replied. "The angels!"

II.

Inside the *Synaxis*, meanwhile, we join the action just as the captain steps up onto the deck after sealing both hatches, and moves to his station just to the left of the entryway. Across from him, on the other side of the entryway, the chaplain is already seated at his station, having inserted the golden ciborium into its receptacle in the center of the Participator while Christopher was securing the hatches. The geometer and the astronomer, both with the hoods of their albs still covering their hair, are likewise seated at their stations, Sophie on Max's side and Maria on Chris's.

All are facing the Participator. As the captain strides to his station, the chaplain and the others rise to chant the revealed activation rite.

> *Glory to the Father and to the Son and to the Holy Spirit,*
>
> *As it was in the beginning, is now, and ever shall be, world without end. Amen.*
>
> *Praise the Lord in the heavens: praise Him in the highest.*
>
> *Praise Him, all ye His angels, praise Him all ye His hosts.*
>
> *Praise Him, O sun and moon; praise Him, all ye stars and light.*
>
> *Praise Him, ye heaven of heavens, and thou water that art above the heavens.*
>
> *Let them praise the name of the Lord; for He spake, and they came to be;*
>
> *He commanded, and they were created....*

As the Metaphysicals chant antiphonally the great psalm of praise, exhorting all creation to praise its Creator, a subtle brightening of the starship's concave interior transpires, although the illumination afforded by the overhead lighting is unchanged By the end of the psalm, when Maxim pulls out his New Testament for the reading, the very air seems noticeably brighter.

Blessed be the God and Father of our Lord Jesus Christ, who has blessed us in Christ with every spiritual blessing in the heavenly places, even as He chose us in Him before the foundation of the world, that we should be holy and blameless before Him.

The apparent brightening of the atmosphere inside the snug polyhedral starship continues throughout the reading from Ephesians, and into the concluding Doxology.

Praise God from whom all blessings flow. Praise Him all creatures here below.

Praise Him above, ye heavenly host. Praise Father, Son, and Holy Ghost. Amen.

By the time the four take their seats after singing the final Amen, the luminosity is such that the captain switches off the overhead lighting, and since there are a few minutes to go before 7:00, they have a moment to acclimate themselves to what they would come to call the "aeviternal ambience" that surrounded them when the *Synaxis* was angelically activated. A "supersensory scintillation" of consciousness itself, an "intellectual tingling", an "ethereal effervescence" of the very senses, all in a kind of "breathless hyperventilation"—such are some of the phrases they would utter in later discussions, as they came to realize that the activation of the vessel, involving its ontological insulation and transport by the angels, had actually transposed them into the habitat of the angels, between time and eternity: the *aeviternum*.

But now, as the ship's clock enters the final countdown, the captain says in a firm and clear voice, "*Synaxis*: Command mode." With barely a perceptible pause, a voice like that of a young boy replies, from the Participator, "Command mode acknowledged." With a significant glance to each of his crew our intrepid metaphysician proceeds, "*Synaxis*: *Alpha-Cygni*." And just like that, the great blue-white supergiant is shining over their heads, the angelic crew projecting its image on the designated squares, having adjusted the ship's distance from the star so that its appearance nearly fills each of the large overhead screens. The view is utterly breathtaking.

Sophie exclaims at once, her alto voice animated with delight, how the color of the blue-white starlight matches the interior paint in the ship, then points out more soberly that this supergiant star has roughly 200 times the diameter, and 50,000 times the luminosity of our sun, and also that it is a variable star, exhibiting non-radial fluctuations with associated spectral shifts. Maria pipes in, the twinkling of her blue eyes only accentuated in the ambience of the angelic field, that the sheer size of the star prompted an adjustment of their location, and that she has corrected the course vector for the next leg of their voyage accordingly. She adds that she intends to query the angels regarding the effect of the star's non-radial variations upon the local geometry of physical spacetime, or vice versa, if the variations are geometrodynamically driven.

But now there is an audible signal from Maxim's notebook,

where he finds the message: "Arise and read: John 1:1-3."
Obediently unfolding his tall frame to its full height, and
producing a small New Testament from a pocket in the
long black cassock, he reads—or rather, chants:

> *In the beginning was the Logos, and the Logos was
> with God, and the Logos was God. He was in the
> beginning with God; all things were made through
> Him, and without Him was not anything made that
> was made.*

As the chaplain completes the reading, a simultaneous gasp
of surprise escapes from all four Metaphysicals, as the visual
appearance of the blue-white supergiant abruptly begins to
vary, as though the brilliant orb is now somehow reflected
within itself, and projected beyond itself, as if it were two or
even three stars, yet still somehow the one same supergiant
star. And not only that. One of these three stars-within-
the-star also displays a paradoxical multiplicity of symbolic
forms comprised within *its* unity, images of all kinds of
creatures from stars to mammals, reflected in this one star,
projected from another, encompassed by a third, yet all
remaining one star, all along. This is the vision our voyagers
behold in the large square screens overhead, of which three
are clearly visible from each station. It is the ship's chaplain
who breaks the rapt silence into which they have fallen.

Maxim: Glory be to God! The angel of Cygnus Alpha has
given us an exegesis, in starlight, of the Gospel I was just
prompted to read. Of course the passage deals explicitly

only with the Father and the Son, God and the Word, but we know from Genesis 1:2 that the Holy Spirit was also *in the beginning, en arche, in principio.* The star comprising the figures of creation clearly signifies the Son, the Logos who contains the *logoi* of all things and therefore through whom all things are made; the star that appears to project the figures is then the unoriginated Father from whom originate the Son and the Spirit, the latter accompanying the former as breath accompanies a word. And all of that in blue-white starlight, presumably composed by the angel of the star and interpreted for display by our crew of angels, for whose yeoman service thanks be to God!

Christopher: Amen to your doxology and thanksgiving, soul brother and chaplain of mine, and not least for your own explanation of the enigmatic vision we behold. Metaphysically, I observe first that here we are still, intellectually, in the uncreated order, namely the Holy Trinity and the uncreated *logoi* or ideas of all things that are to be created. We are not yet considering creation itself. Second, I'd like to adduce an epistemological analogy of my noble namesake the Meister's, whereby he calls the Holy Trinity an "incommensurate sign of Divine Knowledge." This Divine Knowledge is of course God's knowledge of everything, created and uncreated, His omniscience, and in this view the Father is likened to the Knower, the Son to all that is Known (and loved), and the Holy Spirit to the Knowledge itself. As St. Paul wrote to the Corinthians, "the Spirit searches everything, even the depths of God," and "no one comprehends the thoughts of God except the Spirit of God." What are your observations, fair astronomer?

Sophia: First, my dear captain, I am fascinated by the linguistic aspect of the vision, that is, the way it interprets St. John's verses, as noted by my brother, thus confirming the linguistic intelligence of the angels, both of the star itself and of our own crew. Beyond that, I'd like to show you the other four stars we'll be visiting, as viewed from here at Deneb. I've asked the crew to display a wide-angle view looking back toward Earth on the top-center screen and adjacent squares, highlighting our four stars and Earth, or rather Earth's location since the sun is too small to be seen from this distance. You can't miss Sadr in the foreground, only twenty-five light years away and itself a supergiant, and if you look closely, it appears that Sadr has a planet. The other three stars are much farther away, ranging from 1165 (Albireo) to 1475 (Gienah) light years closer to Earth. They appear much smaller than they do from Earth, and do not appear in this perspective as three arms of a cross. But what has our geometer to add?

Maria: Besides being completely amazed by everything that has just transpired, I do have a report from the angels on my question about the geometrical aspects of Deneb's non-radial variability. It seems that the angel of the star, being responsible for governing its motions (including the internal motions which constitute its variability) accomplishes this task by direct intellectual action upon the local geometry of spacetime. In other words the geometry drives the star's variability, and the angel controls the geometry. How elegant! In addition, I should confirm that our course vector to Albireo is optimized and logged in to arrive at a locus between the two stars, a giant and a dwarf, somewhat closer to the dwarf. That's about it for the geometry. I just want to sit here and gaze at this star!

As Maria's discourse comes to an end, the visionary apparition of three-stars-in-one fades into the blue-white brilliance of α-*Cygni*, displayed full-screen and flooding the polyhedral interior of the starship with its light. Then, in that brilliance, appears the icon of an angel, wearing a bright blue robe with white sashes, and adorned with golden halo and wings. The angel's right hand is raised in a gesture of blessing, which after a moment becomes a wave of farewell, and an indication in the general direction of Albireo. This apparent dismissal, with a blessing, is taken well in stride by our Metaphysicals, who are completely drenched in the light of the vision of the Holy Trinity which the angel has afforded them, in the ethereal effervescence of the *aeviternum*. The captain calmly queries the crew as to their readiness for departure, and finding all hands affirmative, initiates the command mode of the starship *Synaxis* and directs her angelic crew to β-*Cygni*, almost 1200 light years closer to Earth.

As before, the transposition is instantaneous. The illumination of the ship's interior decreases perceptibly as the brilliant full-screen images of Deneb disappear, being replaced by two images, about half-screen, of a giant golden-yellow star, and on opposing squares, two corresponding images at perhaps one-tenth screen, of a small but very luminous blue dwarf. The top screen, for the moment, is blank. Our intellectual voyagers, still tingling intellectually with the light they received at Deneb, look with fresh wonder at these new images of the binary system Albireo, displayed in the slant screens overhead. Again it is the astronomer who breaks their silence, her beautiful face beaming over the sheer beauty of the two stars, golden yellow and sapphire blue, and who goes on to report that the golden giant is almost 20 times the sun's diameter, with a luminosity 1200 times greater. The blue dwarf, she adds, is smaller in diameter than the sun but with 230 times the luminosity—a bright little blue dwarf, and a fast-spinning one at that.

But hark! Another signal from the chaplain's tablet and another instruction to read, this time Romans 1:20-21. The chaplain ably complies:

> *Ever since the creation of the world His invisible nature, namely, His eternal power and deity, have been clearly perceived in the things that have been made. So they are without excuse; for although they knew God they did not honor Him as God or give thanks to Him, but they became futile in their thinking and their senseless minds were darkened.*

Perhaps less to their surprise this time, but no less to their amazement, as Maxim resumes his seat there appears in the topmost square overhead a full-screen image of the golden giant Albireo A, which at once begins to display the same trinitarian symbolism of three-stars-as-one, which they just witnessed at Deneb. But as the Metaphysicals recognize what they are seeing, an additional feature appears in the visionary image, a kind of corona of created beings projected or reflected radially around the giant golden three-stars-as-one, brilliantly reflecting the light of the star-as three-stars. The symbolic figures comprised in the Logos-star are seen to be projected into this corona of creatures, as giving them form. But abruptly, a darkening appears on the surface of the creaturely corona, as though the sustaining starlight is no longer clearly reflected—a darkening and a thickening.

Now the whole screen goes black for an instant, and in place of the yellow giant appears the blue dwarf, Albireo B, magnified to about half-screen and with its naturally high spin artificially accelerated in the angelic display. The rapidly-spinning, bright-blue orb develops dark lines of flux across its face, and these flow lines become twisted and entangled, forming vortices with their axes of spin pointing inward toward the dense heart of the dwarf star. The lines thicken, darkening the originally bright face of Albireo B, and then the visionary screen goes dark, leaving the four slant screens displaying both stars on opposite panels. Again, it is the chaplain who speaks first:

Maxim: *Praise the Lord in the heavens! Praise Him in the highest!* The angels of Albireo, like the one of Deneb, are interpreting in light the very verses to which they directed us. Beginning with the earlier astronomical representation of the Trinity, the golden giant is proceeding to signify creation, and to show the origin of creaturely forms in the Son, who is the eternal Logos. This pertains to the first of our two verses. Moreover, the initial radiance of the corona of creatures itself points to their original perfection, which God declared good, and to their being turned toward the source of their being. The darkening and thickening which ensued certainly signifies the Fall, namely the turning of the highest creatures away from the Creator, whence "their senseless minds were darkened". The blue dwarf, it seems to me, takes up the action at this point and focuses on the fallen state, turned in upon itself and away from God, self-centered and at cross-purposes with other selves. At least, that's how I read it. But what says our captain?

Christopher: Praise Him all ye His angels! Praise Him all ye His host! Here we have clearly arrived, metaphysically speaking, in the created order with its original paradisal radiance, and its subsequent corruption because of the angelic rebellion and the ancestral human acquiescence in Satan's proposal. There is probably no need to dwell on the visionary illustration of uncreated *logoi* or ideas of creatures being projected or reflected into the existing creatures themselves, so I'll emphasize the fallen state, which has been notoriously neglected by metaphysicians. According to Genesis the ground is cursed, which covers the mineral kingdom, and mortality has come to the botanical and zoological kingdoms as well as to the human. But only in the latter, created in the image of God, is the fallen nature truly "curved in upon itself" as Max put it, or in Luther's

Latin, *incurvatus in se*—or rather, only in the humans and the rebel angels. For only the intellectual creatures have the capacity to receive the uncreated Light, Knowledge, and Wisdom, because the created intellect is a direct reflection or procession of the uncreated Intellect or eternal Logos. Conversely it is the intellectual creatures who can willfully focus elsewhere, curving the soul toward attachment to created things, and away from the Creator. But I believe our beloved astronomer can direct our attention to created stars, without directing us away from their Creator and ours.

Sophia: *Praise Him, O sun and moon! Praise Him, all ye stars and light!* O captain, my captain, it is again the semantics of the vision, even more than the natural beauty of the stars in closeup, that most fascinates me. It is the way in which the angelic intelligences governing these stars have contrived to signify, in light, a major phase of sacred doctrine according to Scripture! But that said, allow me to point out the view from Albireo. I've tasked the angels to display first the wide-angle view toward Earth, in which you can see the sun 385 light years away, as well as the next two stars on our course, δ- and ε-*Cygni*, the former a little over 200 light years away and the latter a little over 300. Now looking back out toward Deneb, we see only that star and Sadr, our final stop before home, both nearly 1200 light years away, and both noticeably brighter than they appear from Earth. And zooming in now on Delta, our next destination, we see a trinary system comprising a blue-white subgiant, a smaller yellow-white star, and an orange dwarf orbiting them at a distance. That's about it for astronomy: what says our gentle geometer?

Maria: Praise Him, ye heavens of heavens, and ye waters that art above the heavens! Let them praise the name of the Lord, for He spake, and they came to be! He commanded, and they were created! And He created also the firmament of spacetime, in which centers of gravitational curvature amassing matter-energy are induced by uncreated *logoi*, forming stars. The geometry of physical spacetime controls the formation of structures of matter-energy, but the formally causative geometries are induced intellectually by the action of uncreated ideas or *logoi* in Christ. Regarding our current position, we are in a spacetime location abstracted from motion in the time dimension, ontologically insulated from the physical spacetime in which we are situated, precisely on a line between the two stars although not equidistant. Let us recall that the light leaving these stars at this moment will arrive at Earth at the same time we do, just as the light leaving Delta when we arrive there will do. The spatial component of our location at Delta will be on a line perpendicular to the line between the two brighter stars, and terminating at the distant dwarf. So that's the geometry report. What's next, skipper?

The captain observes that they are probably all a bit overwhelmed by the luminous illustrations of *sacra doctrina* to which the angels have treated them, and that perhaps they should pause for a moment to reflect further on what they have witnessed. But all at once the stellar orbs of the golden giant and the sapphire dwarf appear full-screen overhead, and within each orb an angelic form, each robed in the color of its star, like two holy icons. Their hands are raised in a gesture of blessing which, as at Deneb, becomes a wave of farewell. Smiling gallantly at each of the others, and receiving equally gallant smiles in return, captain Eckhart of the starship *Synaxis* directs his angelic crew to relocate the vessel to the designated location at δ-*Cygni*.

III.

All of the screens go dark for an instant, then begin shining with new images: of the four slant screens, two display the blue-white subgiant Delta A, while on the opposing two squares shines the yellow-white Delta B, and on the top screen the dim orange dwarf. The image of the subgiant is nearly full-screen, while the other two stars are scaled in proportion to their diameters, roughly quarter- and tenth-screen. The supersensory scintillations of the aeviternal ambience, in which they are subsisting, undoubtedly serve to heighten the sensory experience of the stellar images projected by the crew of angels, and Sophia cannot conceal her delight in what she calls the astronomer's paradise into which God and her beloved captain have brought her, as she conducts her preliminary briefing. The subgiant A, she explains, is only five times the solar diameter in size, but shines with over 150 times the solar luminosity, while yellow-white B is only one-and-a-half times the sun's diameter with six times its luminosity. The orange dwarf

C, she continues, is just over half the sun's diameter, and its luminosity less than the sun's. The dwarf orbits widely around the other two stars, and from either of them it appears about the size of Deneb in the sky of Earth. Our astronomer is just beginning to congratulate the angels on their artistry in displaying the three stars, when the chaplain's tablet again signals the arrival of a lectionary instruction, this time Luke 2:9-11. Maxim arises and chants from the leatherbound Testament:

> *And an angel of the Lord appeared to them, and the glory of the Lord shone around them, and they were filled with fear. And the angel said to them, "Be not afraid; for behold I bring you good news of a great joy which will come to all the people; for to you is born this day in the city of David a Savior, who is Christ the Lord.*

By now our Metaphysicals have been schooled to expect an exegesis, in light, of this Nativity text so familiar to their ears, and the angels who form the operative power of the spacecraft do not disappoint them. The original images of the three stars vanish, and the slant screens going dark, the blue-white subgiant appears in the top screen, looking much like a twin of supergiant Deneb, both stars having been scaled to the same screen. And just like that other blue-white star, and subsequently the golden giant of Albireo, Delta first displays by reflection and projection the figure of three-stars-in-one, including representations of the *logoi* in the reflected orb. This time, however, one of the myriad *logoi* stands out from all the rest, represented by a gleaming blood-red cross in marked contrast to the blue-white brilliance of the star. But now the stellar background changes from blue-white to yellow-white as Delta B takes the place of its subgiant partner, maintaining the same symbolic signature of Trinity and *logoi*, with one *logos* singled out, but proceeding to display the corona of creatures and its darkening by the Fall. As our Metaphysicals watch with wonder the darkened surface of the orb, the gleam of the blood-red cross burns through, shining brightly in its midst and sending ripples of light across the darkened face of the visionary star—which suddenly shrinks to about quarter-screen, showing dull orange through the encrustations of darkness, some of which thicken to form a grey cross. Now, with equal suddenness, the crossed and shrunken star expands to full-screen, simultaneously brightening to the blue-white brightness of Delta A once more, still with tenuous networks of darkness writhing across the face of the orb, but with continuous ripples of light from the heart of the star-as-three-stars sweeping invincibly over the dark encrustations. As the visionary sequence fades, and as the astronomical display of Delta A, B and C returns to the screens, three sets of eyes turn to the chaplain.

Maxim: *Glory to God in the highest!* Let us connect some theological dots here, and consider what these stars have been showing us. The vision at Deneb was entirely of the uncreated order, portraying the text from St. John's prologue; then Albireo, while recapitulating the former, added the corona of creatures and the darkening due to their rebellion, reflecting St. Paul's passage on the evidence of the Creator in creation, and the angelic and human rebellion that refuses to honor Him. What the angels of Cygnus Delta, with the able assistance of our crew, have just shown us is perfectly continuous with the previous visions, but showing now the uncreated *logos* of Jesus (the gleaming ruby cross in the orb of the *logoi*}, His becoming incarnate in the Nativity (the cross burning through the darkness, his crucifixion (the grey cross on the orange dwarf), and his resurrection and ascension (the resurgence of light in the final image). It is tempting to extrapolate what phase of Christian doctrine the angel of Gienah has in mind, but I will resist the temptation, and instead ask the captain for his take.

Christopher: Hosanna in the highest! I too will refrain from anticipating what Epsilon has in store for us, and I have nothing to add to your theological analysis, but I would like to comment on the metaphysics of the *logos* of Jesus as an individual creature, and also on the interior aspect of the Nativity, or birth of the Word. The fascinating thing about the first point is that the actual Person of the man Jesus is the uncreated Second Person of the Holy Trinity, who is Christ our Lord, the eternal Logos in whom are the uncreated *logoi* of all creatures, including the creature named Jesus of Nazareth. Since the *logos* of Jesus specifies the human nature that is united with the divine nature in the Person of Christ, that logos must be unique in its relation to this Person, who indeed eternally comprises all the *logoi*, but only this one In such a way as to incarnate it as a created being, in Person. On the other point, my namesake the Meister and Martin Luther alike spoke of the birth of the Word in the heart, or *spiritus*, or ground of the soul, with the Meister speaking in terms of the inversion of created intellect into the uncreated Intellect from which it proceeds, thus transposing the soul into Christ, and Luther speaking in terms of the Word indwelling the *spiritus* or heart by faith, which finds itself outside itself (*raptus*) in Christ. But now, as we continue to contemplate the cosmic catechesis through which we are being conducted, I invite my brown-eyed astronomer to report.

Sophia: *Glory to the newborn King!* I honestly don't know whether our Lord is more glorified by the visual beauty of these three stars, blue-white, yellow-white and orange, as displayed by our angels; or by the visionary illustration of His Nativity presented by the angels of the stars, not to mention the events at the end of His incarnate life. *Praise Him, all ye His angels!* On the astronomy front, the view from δ-*Cygni* is displayed first looking out toward Deneb and Sadr, over 1400 light years from here, while Albireo is visible in the foreground, just over 200 light years away. And turning our view now in toward Earth's sun at 170 light years, we see Gienah or ε-*Cygni*, which is of course where we are headed next, 100 light years closer to that sun. Gienah is an orange giant which emits two distinct stellar spectra, a phenomenon I hope to investigate during our visit. But I detect a twinkle in the eyes of our geometer, to whom I gladly yield the deck.

Maria: *The Lord is King, He is clothed with majesty!* Infinite and all-possible Intellect, His thoughts are higher than our thoughts, His geometry higher than our geometry, and according to these He fashions all things; yet He allows us to participate in His thinking, by glimpses, and these precious glimpses are our own truest thinking. He has stretched out this physical firmament of spacetime and located stars in it, in such a way that geometrical analysis can define vectors originating at a desired location in the vicinity of one star or system, and terminating in the vicinity of another. Zeroing in on our present location on a line perpendicular to the line between Delta A and B, and terminating at C, posed a complicated problem, but the Creator had the geometry exactly right, and was kind enough to let me have a look, with the help of an angel, I'm sure. By contrast our vector to Gienah, a simpler target, was easy to set up. Now again, if these three angels will give us one breathless moment to reflect on their luminous teaching, and to contemplate the natural beauty of their stars, that is exactly what I would love to do.

The others agree whole-heartedly that they too would not at all mind the opportunity to ponder what they have seen, and maybe even hazard some speculations as to how the angel of Gienah will round out the interstellar tableau of doctrine through which they are being conducted. The angels, however, have other ideas, as their images in the orbs of their corresponding stars go full-screen: one robed in blue with white sash, another in yellow with white sash, and the third in orange with sash of grey—all with wings and halos gleaming gold. Simultaneously the three angels raise their hands of light in the now-familiar gesture of blessing, and of dismissal. With unfailing gallantry and thumbs-up all around from his human crewmates, the captain initiates "command mode" and instructs his crew of angels to teleport *Synaxis* to ε-*Cygni*, called Gienah, the "wing".

In the aethereal effervescence of their experience, while subsisting in the *aeviternam* of the angels, the orb of the orange giant appears simultaneously on all five screens, scaled to half-screen on the four slants and full-screen overhead. Sophie's big brown eyes are wide with wonder as she looks from the image of the giant orange star to her notebook, explaining that she is initiating a query as to its double spectrum, and adding that in size, Gienah is 11 times the sun's diameter and shines with 62 times its luminosity. She goes on to explain that Gienah was long considered a multiple star system, because seen from Earth it has two apparent companions, one in the distance behind it and another comoving, but not gravitationally bound; besides being itself a "spectroscopic double." This latter feature, she says, could be interpreted from Earth as two stars overlapping in the telescopic images in which the two spectra are detected, but since they can now confirm from close-up that Gienah is indeed only one star, the problem of the two spectra is especially perplexing. The astronomer pauses with an enigmatic smile, just as her brother's tablet signals the arrival of the angelic message specifying the text for the present phase of their experience: Matthew 24: 30-31.

> *Then will appear the sign of the Son of Man in heaven, and then all the tribes of the earth will mourn, and they will see the Son of Man coming on the clouds of heaven with power and great glory; and He will send out His angels with a loud trumpet call, and they will gather the elect from the four winds, from one end of heaven to the other.*

As Maxim's deep baritone finishes chanting these lines from the "little apocalypse," attributed to Jesus Himself, the full-screen image of the orange giant overhead begins, as if in slow motion, to recapitulate in detail the luminous symbolism of Christian doctrine as developed by the angels of Deneb, Albireo, and Delta. The reflection of the stellar orb within itself and its projection beyond itself, three-stars-in one-star, one of them comprising the figures of created beings signifying the uncreated *logoi* of all creatures, with one of these figures standing out from all the others; the corona of creatures actualizing the uncreated ideas in God, initially radiant as if reflecting and projecting the radiance of divine Being, then darkening and thickening as denoting the Fall; the burning of the figure of Jesus in fiery light through thickening darkness, initiating circles and waves of light criss-crossing the darkened face of the orb— every previous phase is meticulously, slowly, and clearly repeated. Suddenly the entire face of the visionary orb is quartered, as a bright orange cross extending to its edges burns through the encrusted darkness, dividing it into four diminishing wedges. At the very center of the fiery cross appears the figure of Jesus in pure white, surrounded by legions of angels, one of whom is seen to stand forth, raise two trumpets to his mouth, and blow a strange but stirring call that is audible inside *Synaxis*. At this call, rings of angels sweep over the diminishing quarters of darkness, gathering and bringing toward the center shining figures of human souls in their resurrection bodies, all gathering in circles around the Son of Man as the last of the fallen darkness disappears in flame. This visionary image remains displayed overhead as the ship's chaplain, surveying it steadily with his dark eyes, begins his commentary.

Maxim: *Kyrie eleison! Lord have mercy!* Although we have prudently refrained from sharing any speculations on the subject, we all must have suspected some portrayal of the End of Time would follow the development at Delta, which terminated on the level of doctrine with our Lord's Resurrection and Ascension, and the lights of the Church militant flickering defiantly in mitigation of the darkness. This is of course the phase in which Earth was as we left it, and still is as we intend to return to it, so the vision with which Gienah is blowing our minds as we speak represents the Coming of our Lord for which Earth still waits. Observe that, just as our text from Matthew focuses on the gathering of the elect, leaving unmentioned the fate of the children of darkness, so the vision illustrates only the gathering, leaving the destruction of the darkness in flame to signify the fate of the unregenerate. And lastly, since only one more stop remains on our pilgrimage through outer space, I shall hazard a prediction of the general character of our vision at Sadr: for what comes after the End of Time but Eternal Life, the Heavenly City, the Paradise of the saints in Light? But what has our metaphysical captain to say?

Christopher: Christe eleison! Christ have mercy! I confess to feeling a particular poignancy at this phase, which touches so closely upon our own earthly futures, so far as the signs seem to indicate. But the metaphysician in me cannot help wondering about St. Peter's words regarding the "day of the Lord": how the elements will be melted or dissolved with fire, the Earth burned up, and the heavens kindled and dissolved so that the new heavens and new earth can appear. It is hard to know exactly what concept of "elements" St. Peter or his scribe may have in mind, but since, metaphysically, an element is most simply the "primary component of each being", and since the primary components of all matter in the universe are the chemical elements as we know them, from hydrogen to uranium etc., let us consider these chemical elements as being dissolved with fire. Not the fire of oxidation as we know it on Earth, like wood burning, but the fire of nuclear chemistry unleashed, dissolving the atomic nuclei into protons and neutrons in a sea of electrons, and even dissolving these in a supernatural burst of pure energy. Simultaneously, the eternal *logoi* of the elect and of all creatures to be manifest in the new creation are irradiated with *esse gloriae*, the uncreated being of glory, bringing into existence the new heavens and the new earth. At present, however, we are still in the old creation, atoms and all, even though ontologically insulated from our physical environment. Which brings us to our astronomer's report.

Sophia: *Kyrie eleison! Lord have mercy!* By your leave, my dear captain, I'd like to begin with a word on semantics, the conveyance of meaning by the symbolic order of figures portrayed in the light of this orange giant. The angel of Gienah, together with our outboard crew, has not only accurately recapitulated the doctrinal phases portrayed by the previous stars, but signified brilliantly the text from Matthew it was to illuminate. I also observe that this is the first of the visions to include an audible component, namely the curious but compelling call of the angel with the dual trumpets, which oddly enough may well be a clue to the problem of Gienah's double spectrum. What I mean, is that it occurs to me that the generation of starlight with a specific spectrum by the angel of the star, which we have been able to interpret linguistically, could also be interpreted as music. In this analogy the generation of a double spectrum could be signified by its angel playing two horns, which makes me wonder if the angel of Gienah has inserted himself into the vision, as a kind of signature. But enough speculation. The view from Gienah is the closest we've had of the sun, and with zoom-in the Earth is actually visible from here, just 72 light years away. Now turning our view outward to our next destination, Sadr or γ-*Cygni*, we see it and Deneb almost 1500 light years distant, not much brighter than they appear from Earth, and in the foreground Delta and Albireo. Sadr, as we shall shortly see, is a yellow-white supergiant at the center of the Cross, in the heart of the Swan, and as you will recall we discovered a planet in orbit around it, from our vantage at Deneb. But what says our genial geometer?

Maria: *Christe eleison! Christ have mercy!* Despite being utterly awestruck by the apocalyptic vision over our heads, I've been running a couple of queries involving harmonic analysis of spectral elements within and across the two spectra, and what the crew is coming up with is a pair of parallel representations of purely intellectual operations on astrodynamic functions, geometrically distributed throughout the body of the star. The modulations of starlight controlled by these functions determine the spectra emitted, so by intellectual operation on these functions the angel induces two parallel representations corresponding to the two spectra, which can indeed be configured as music. So I can substantiate Sophie's notion of the angel as "playing two horns." Regarding my slightly more pedestrian office of charting our course to Sadr, I have asked the crew to adjust our spatial coordinates of arrival to position us close to the planet at Sophie's request, even though we have no instruction about the planet, at least yet. Our time coordinate is unaltered, namely the time at which the starlight leaving Sadr will arrive at Earth when we do, like with the earlier stars. So that's about it for the geometry. Suppose we'll get hustled off again?

The stunning apocalyptic vision which remained shining

over their heads during these discourses, now reverts to the natural view of the orange giant, in which appears, like a living icon, the angel of Gienah, robed in bright orange with a purple sash, and bearing two horns, one in each fiery hand. The angel raises both horns to his mouth and plays audibly, not the apocalyptic call played in the vision, but a kind of sonata, a veritable recital of two-part melodies, providing our Metaphysicals with a lingering moment to consider the course over which this voyage has so swiftly carried them. In addition to a series of stunning astronomical close-ups and several scientific discoveries, they have been treated to four visionary tableaux essentially summarizing the Christian doctrine as expressed in the Creeds, with certain metaphysical details included. The Lord summoned them into outer space at the End of Time, bringing with them a consecrated eucharistic host housed in the very core of their vessel, with the understanding that the first four stars were to prepare them spiritually for the fifth. At Maxim's suggestion they join in meditation on the chief points of the doctrine: The uncreated Trinity, whose Second Person, the Son, contains the eternal *logoi* of all creatures including the creature as which He will incarnate; Creation of the creatures corresponding to the *logoi*, their original perfection, and their Fall; Incarnation of the Son, His Crucifixion, Resurrection, and Ascension; and Return or Second Coming of the Son. As they hold this doctrine in their minds, stimulated by the intellectual tingling characteristic of the *aeviternum*, the angel concludes his recital, silently putting aside his two horns, and now raises his fiery hands in the gesture of blessing, and of dismissal.

Fortified by their catechetical meditation, and by their breathless anticipation of the climax of their mission in the heart of the Swan, the four are of one mind in their readiness for whatever Sadr may hold, as captain Eckhart initiates command mode and issues the designated order: "*Synaxis*: γ-*Cygni*."

CHAPTER FIVE:
THE LAKE IN THE HEART
OF THE SWAN

I.

As the starship *Synaxis* blinks into existence at the designated spacetime location near Sadr and its planet, the interior illumination of the vessel changes, in an instant of darkness, from orange to yellow-white. Two of the slant screens overhead display a full-screen image of the massive star, while the other two offer a view of the beautiful planet, scaled to one-third screen-size. The top screen assumes a perspective several light-minutes from the ship, showing their position relative to the star and the planet, namely "alongside" the latter at a distance of about ten planetary diameters, and the same distance from Sadr as is the planet. The reader can imagine the scale of their view of the planet as comparable to viewing a globe, twelve inches in dimeter, from ten feet away. All this, with the unearthly music of the angel of Gienah still fresh in their memories, not to mention their concentrated meditation on the doctrine of faith—these phases of experience succeeding each other not as moments of time but as intelligible forms, according to the ambience of the *aeviternum*.

The big brown eyes of the ship's astronomer appear wider than ever as she reports the basic astronomical data on this yellow-white supergiant star, 150 times the radius of the sun and 33,000 times its luminosity, with a solar spectrum and surrounded by a diffuse nebulosity of interstellar dust in which new stars appear to be forming. Like Deneb, moreover, Sadr is moving toward Earth. But it is the planet which is chiefly responsible for the apparent magnitude of those brown eyes, for not only is its image, as displayed on the screens by the angels, surpassingly beautiful, but by simple queries to the latter she has gleaned a few essentials about the planetary orbit, diameter, gravity, and geography. Because of the star's size and mass the planet orbits at twelve times the Earth-Sun distance (12 AUs or astronomical units), and although its diameter is about one-quarter larger than Earth's, its mass and therefore gravity are only around two-thirds of Earth's. Geographically there is one great continent covering roughly a third of the planetary surface, the balance being one vast ocean. On the continent is a central highland with a large inland lake, from which rivers run in four directions, branching out to irrigate the entire continent. This is what has so excited our astronomer.

But now the brilliant images of the yellow-white supergiant begin to display the iconic form of the angel of Sadr, arrayed in a robe of gleaming gold with white sash, and with halo and wings also golden. To their great surprise, the angel addresses them audibly:

Sadr: Peace be unto you, and greetings. My fellow spirits inform me that y'all have fared well under their instruction. It is my office to examine y'all before you proceed. First then, Christopher, what is the nature of faith?

Christopher: As Dante to St. Peter's posing of this question, in the former poet's *Paradiso*, I begin with the Apostle's definition in Hebrews: Faith is the substance of things hoped for, the evidence of things unseen. But Dante considered "substance" (Latin *substantia*) only in the aspect of "standing under," hence belief as the foundation of our hope, whereas I would point out that the original Greek word translated "*substantia*" or "substance" is actually *hypostasis*. This is a metaphysical term for a being that subsists in itself, a thing that actually exists, and theologically it is the term translated "person" in the doctrines of the Trinity and the Incarnation. Since Christ is the Second Hypostasis of the Holy Trinity, and hypostatically unites His divine and human natures, I interpret St. Paul's definition in reference to faith as the indwelling of Christ, who contains all that we hope for and assures us of what we cannot see.

Sadr: Well answered, Christopher. Now Maxim, what are the sources of this saving faith?

Maxim: The Holy Spirit pours the golden light of intellect over the sacred texts, the Scriptures Old and New, reflecting in the human heart an understanding of God's revelation, which like a rational seed takes root as faith. The source of faith is thus the Holy Spirit, Third Hypostasis of the Holy Trinity, who inspired the human authors of the Scriptures to record God's revelation truly, and who inspires us who read and hear it to understanding its faith-generating doctrine.

Sadr: Eloquently spoken, Maxim. Now let me direct a question to Maria: For what reason do you accept the divine truth of Scripture?

Maria: The strong coherence of the Testaments, the Old prophesying what the New reports as manifest, and glorified from Virgin Birth to Resurrection and Ascension by miracles of feeding, healing, and audible testimonies from heaven—this I would call evidence of Scripture's truth. As further evidence I would cite the miracle of Pentecost and the subsequent miraculous growth of the Church, as well as her endurance against all odds, even unto the End. But there's an underlying certainty, a hypostatic presence in the heart, of Christ Himself by act of the Holy Spirit. This certitude outweighs all evidence.

Sadr: Marvelously confessed, Maria. Finally, I ask Sophia to summarize the doctrine of the faith we all confess.

Sophia: We believe in one eternal Creator of all beings and forms, for whose reality we find evidence in the sciences of nature, and arguments in the science of being, which is

Christopher's discipline. We also believe this Creator exists as a Trinity of Hypostases or Persons, the Father unoriginate, the Son begotten, and the Holy Spirit proceeding; and that the Person of the Son unites His divine nature with human nature in order to incarnate as Jesus. These things we believe not because of metaphysics or the sciences, but because they are revealed in the Scriptures, where we understand them by the Holy Spirit, as my brother has explained, and where like a seed, or a spark, or a star in heaven, this principial doctrine shines in our hearts.

Sadr: Superbly summarized, Sophia. Do y'all now in unison confess your affirmation of faith according to all that y'all have said?

Metaphysicals: We do. Amen.

Sadr: *Te Deum laudamus*! Clearance to proceed is hereby granted. But now I must inform y'all on *how* you are to proceed, which is as follows. I have instructed your operating crew to target a landing site on my planet Sadronia, the coordinates of which are available on your information system. Upon landing, the crew will deactivate the ontological shield so that you can disembark. Transportation will be provided to a site on the shore of the Great Lake, where your mission will be accomplished. You will return to this location for debriefing after you are dismissed by our Lord. Finally, when you disembark from the ship, Maxim is to remove the ciborium from its bezel and take it to the lakeside. Everything else you need to know will be provided.

And now, blessed ones, allow me to chant four verses from our Lord's Revelation to St. John:

> *And in the Spirit he carried me away to a great, high mountain, and showed me the holy city Jerusalem coming down out of heaven from God, having the glory of God, its radiance like a most rare jewel, like a jasper, clear as crystal. ... Then he showed me the river of the water of life, bright as crystal, flowing from the throne of God and of the Lamb through the middle of the street of the city ...*

As the gold-robed angel finishes chanting the prophetic text, he raises his arms and intones, "*The Lord be with you,*" to which our Metaphysicals spontaneously reply, "*And with you, spirit.*" The dialogue continues:

> *Lift up your hearts. / We lift them to the Lord.*
>
> *Let us give thanks to the Lord our God. / It is right to give Him thanks and praise.*

The angel concludes: "It is truly meet, right and salutary that I now and hereby direct y'all on your way. Amen. *Synaxis*: Sadronia."

II.

Our Metaphysicals' first clue that their stalwart starship

had landed on the planet the angel called Sadronia, is a slight sensation of settling as the blue polyhedron nestles into the shallow declivity selected by the angelic crew. Almost simultaneously, the overhead panels go to window mode, the slant screens showing treetops and the top screen a sky as blue as Earth's, suggesting that they have landed in a forest clearing. But now the screens go dark as the angels deactivate the vessel, and the captain switches on the cabin lights before descending below deck to unseal the hatches, while the chaplain removes the golden ciborium from the core of the Participator. As Christopher opens the outer hatch, sliding the panel to one side, a gentle breeze of unmistakable fragrance wafts in and upward to the deck space, eliciting cries of delight from Sophie and Maria: "Roses!" Following their captain's lead, the crew descends to the open hatch and emerges onto a grassy field, bright green with thick sod, which is indeed surrounded on all sides by a forest of tall evergreens, and surmounted by a deep blue sky that could be mistaken for Earth's.

And yet the comparison is imperfect, because first of all the supersensory scintillations and intellectual tingling, which they experienced inside *Synaxis* when activated, did not subside when they emerged into the delicious fresh air of Sadronia. Second the grass, the trees, the sky, the very air give the impression of being the originals, the archetypes of which their kinds on Earth are but corrupted copies. Rapt in such paradisal impressions, accentuated even more by the lightness of body afforded by Sadronia's lower gravity, the four gaze in wonderment upon the sheer beauty of the place, noticing now the hedges of rose that border the clearing, broken only by several trails emerging from the forest. An observer at the edge of the clearing, which is not over 150 yards across, would behold a scene most picturesque at this moment: in the center of the rich green field stands the celestial blue polyhedron, as if reflecting the deep blue sky overhead, and in the foreground four human figures, three robed in white and one in black, lifting up their hands in thanksgiving and making little leaps of surprising height, all framed by towering evergreens and ringed with abundant yellow-white roses.

But now, upon this intriguing scene, enter four white unicorns with golden horns, through one of the breaks in the hedge, rapidly covering the distance to our astonished Metaphysicals, each of whom is quickly singled out by the approach, with a slight bow, of one of the unicorns. Each unicorn kneels in a clear invitation to mount, and since all of our voyagers are excellent equestrians, the invitations are swiftly and nimbly accepted, despite the unaccustomed riding attire of albs and sandals. All mounted, the four unicorns make one circle around *Synaxis*, prancing and bounding playfully while their riders accustom themselves to their fabulous steeds, grasping their white manes as necessary. Then, four abreast, they break into a gallop toward the trailhead from which they emerged, again quickly closing the distance, and falling into double file as they enter the forest through the break in the rose hedge. The unicorns have so arranged themselves that Christopher and Sophia are riding side by side, as likewise Maxim and

Maria behind them, each startling stride of this low-gravity gallop carrying them farther, and higher, than possible for any horse on Earth.

Quickly adapting to the unearthly gait, our Metaphysicals are filled with delight at the grandeur of the primeval forest through which this broad trail runs, with great thick trunks towering into a high canopy of green, like columns in a cathedral—and doubly delighted to be making this ride, each at the side of his or her beloved. The forest is also filled with songs of birds, a few of whose colorful forms can be seen flitting among the massive trunks, or perched in the canopy. Suddenly the trail emerges into an upland clearing with only a few scattered trees, but myriads of multicolored flowers with clouds of butterflies, and a large herd of white horses. They also notice a brightening sky in the direction in which they are riding: the deep blue of the Sadronian firmament which had greeted them on landing, is indeed brightening in the direction toward which the unicorns are carrying them, the direction in which those golden horns are pointing as they once again plunge into the shade of the forest. Another exhilarating gallop through these stately woods, albs and cassock fluttering gracefully with the long, high strides of their steeds, and the party emerges on a broad sandy beach along the shore of the Great Lake.

As though the vast sheet of still water is not sufficiently breathtaking, just over the surface of the lake rises the radiant orb of Sadr, appearing slightly larger and brighter than the Sun on Earth, yet not proportionately hotter on their faces. Forming again four abreast, the unicorns trot smartly along the sand toward what appears to be a low stone table by the lake, alongside of which two human figures are seen standing, both wearing red robes under green mantles. By now the gently brilliant light of Sadr has completely transfigured the blue sky of Sadronia's night to a radiant yellow-white, and a low reverberation arises over the lake, which turns out to be the trumpeting of swans, a myriad of swans. The unicorns halt at a respectful distance from the stone table and the two long-bearded old men, and kneel for their riders to dismount. They then retire to a distance, leaving our Metaphysicals face to face with the two venerable men, both of whom raise their right hands in a gesture of peace.

The trumpeting of the swans, now visibly converging in large V's on the spot, has grown so loud as to render verbal communication impossible, when suddenly as the converging flocks settle onto the Lake before them, the whole host of the trumpeting swans suddenly goes silent. The cause of their silence is not long in coming, for right from the direction of Sadr's brilliant orb, as though hiding in its glare, appears an exceptionally large white swan with a small figure riding on its back. The giant swan lands on the still water with perfect grace, paddling placidly to the shore, where the diminutive passenger slides deftly off its back and steps lightly ashore, proceeding with dignity to the low stone table.

The four Metaphysicals and the two venerable men fall to

their knees before the Child, whom Christopher recognizes at once and whose identity the others quickly infer. Standing on the order of four feet tall, the Child is arrayed in high-priestly garb of golden robe with white sleeves, and a long white sash embroidered with gold crosses, extending over both shoulders, down the front and around His waist. His face is that of an intelligent seven-year-old boy, but with a supernatural radiance illuminating this boyish countenance, an expression kind and yet serious. He gestures to Maxim, who somehow understands that he is to place the golden ciborium on the stone table, an office he quickly and reverently carries out. The Child raises His hands and lifts up His countenance in a gesture of invocation, then leans forward and picks up the ciborium from the table, holding it with both hands before His chest, where the shoulder sashes meet the frontal.

Suddenly, on both sides of the Child and behind Him, a veritable host of angels appears, as though composing a living icon of their Synaxis around the Child. Indeed, as our Metaphysicals fall back a few steps in awe, rising from their knees along with the venerable duo, they notice a six-winged seraph crouched beneath the table, completing the composition, just as the whole heavenly host breaks into the *Sanctus*, with instrumental accompaniment by the assembled swans.

> *Holy! Holy! Holy! Lord God of Hosts, Heaven and Earth are full of your glory!*

Hosannah in the Highest! Blessed is He who cometh in the Name of the Lord!

Hosannah in the Highest!

The humans immediately join the familiar chant, bowing before the Child until the "Blessed is He", then making the sign of the cross while returning to upright, to gaze again at the diminutive High Priest, still holding the golden ciborium before Him.

As the colossal chorus of the *Sanctus* fades to silence over the still Lake, even the swans are motionless as the priestly Child steps lightly from behind the stone table, removing the top from the ciborium and producing a tiny gold spoon from one sleeve. Our Metaphysicals are standing In a row facing the table, in the order in which the unicorns deposited them, with the mantled ancients standing one on each end. The Child stops before one of the latter, holding up a golden spoonful of entincted host dipped from the ciborium, and saying, "This is my Body and Blood, given and shed for you." After the first of the ancients receives the Sacrament in this extraordinary manner, the Child proceeds along the row, communing the four Metaphysicals and the other of the ancients in the same manner. He then returns, with solemn strides, to the table, where facing the communicants, He says, "May the Body and Blood of your Lord Jesus Christ, I in you and you in Me, strengthen and preserve you unto eternal life. Amen."

At this He turns, carrying the ciborium to the edge of the lake, and stooping down in the sand, he painstakingly rinses the ciborium in the water, three times, which precipitates the most remarkable phenomenon, or sequence of phenomena. From the spot where the Child rinsed the residue from the ciborium, a sort of golden shimmering spreads radially over the surface of the lake, which is already yellow-white in appearance, reflecting the daytime sky of Sadronia. Over the face of these already-radiant waters, the golden shimmering initiated by the Child's action spreads in waves to the horizon, lending a luster of gold to the vast body of water. The Child now refills the ciborium with the transfigured water, replaces the top, and rises to His feet, still facing the lake. Far out across the golden surface, perhaps a mile offshore, a sudden upthrust of waves is seen, and not of waves only, but of a massive foursquare structure rising majestically out of the lake.

As water streams from the rising structure, the likeness of a great walled city becomes apparent, gleaming like pure gold yet somehow clear as glass, and as it rises to full height, roughly equal to its breadth, huge foundation stones become visible, each of a different color and glowing like gigantic gemstones. A central gate appears in the wall facing the shore, opening to reveal a broad golden street running through the middle of the city. At its far end stands an elevated throne, radiant with glory. Out from beneath the throne pours a veritable torrent, clear as crystal, forming a river that runs right down the middle of the transparent golden street and out the central gate into the lake.

The Child turns to face the humans, a broad boyish smile on his shining face, and after depositing the refilled ciborium on the table, He raises His hands in benediction. Then turning again to the lake, He steps lightly down to the edge where His great swan awaits. Nimbly He mounts the winged steed, which promptly leaps into the air, catching itself on its wings like a heron, and flies directly down the lake toward the city. At this the whole host of swans point their beaks in the same direction and take flight behind the Child, trumpeting gloriously as they go, while our Metaphysicals, flanked by the mantled ancients, watch frozen in wide-eyed amazement.

As if on cue, the ancients take several steps forward, then turn to face the two young couples, and introduce themselves: he who stands before Christopher and Sophia, as Enoch, and he who faces Maxim and Maria, as Elijah. Standing thus face to face with the patriarch and the prophet, who appear as if they have just stepped out of an icon, our Metaphysicals begin to wonder whether *they* have stepped into one. Speaking slowly and by turns, Enoch and Elijah first instruct Christopher and Maxim to return the golden ciborium to its place in the starship, where it will serve the same function as before. Further, the ciborium is to be kept in place in the vessel after their return to Earth, and is in no circumstance to be opened without specific instructions.

When this practical matter has been communicated, and the ciborium secured in a pocket of Maxim's cassock, Enoch steps forward, taking the right hands of the captain and his astronomer, and joins them between his own hands. Elijah does the same with the chaplain and his geometer, and then speaking in unison and smiling benevolently, the two mantled ancients solemnly inform the young couples that their Lord desires them, when they return to Earth, to marry and bear children. With that they lay their hands on the four young heads and bless them all. Stepping back, they then summon the four unicorns, which come cantering briskly down the beach and kneel to be mounted.

The unicorns convey the dazed and delighted young people back toward their spacecraft by a different route, much of it unforested open prairie adorned with various flowers, and with large herds of white horses galloping joyfully or grazing placidly on the lush grasses. The golden-horned steeds, running two abreast with the now-betrothed couples riding side by side, reduce their gait to a sort of bounding trot as they draw near one of the herds of horses, which appear to be moving in ranks and practicing maneuvers. Suddenly, in the supersensory scintillations of the ambience there appears a cadre of angels, visibly involved in directing the movements of the horses in orderly ranks and formations. Having given our starstruck voyagers a moment to absorb this scene, the unicorns again quicken their gait, enter a trail into the forest, and soon emerge into the rose-bordered clearing they had left just before daybreak. They circle the blue polyhedron, its color no longer matching the sky but immeasurably more brilliant in Sadronia's daylight, then forming four abreast, they trot up to the hatch side and kneel.

Dismounting on cue, the four watch with continuing wonder as the fabulous creatures bow gracefully, then then wheel and gallop in long, high strides to one of the trailheads, vanishing into the forest beyond. For an undefinable moment the Metaphysicals stand motionless, breathing deeply the rose-scented air and absorbing the sequence of experiences they have so swiftly undergone, when both at once, Sophia and Maria throw their arms around Christopher and Maxim, respectively, and are immediately met with enthusiastic embraces and kisses. After a moment of smiles all around, the captain dutifully reminds his astronomer, chaplain, and geometer that they need to board the ship and return to location at Sadr, as instructed. The order is acknowledged readily enough, and the ladies board first while the chaplain installs the ciborium in the Participator, and the captain carefully closes and seals both hatches before ascending to take his place on deck. This done, he is informed by the geometer that the course vector for their return to the original Sadr-location is duly logged in, and immediately proceeds with the usual verbal commands, *Synaxis* responding exactly as before.

III.

Our Metaphysicals experience a literal *déjà vu* as they

reenter the exact spacetime location from which they've previously departed for their adventure on Sadronia, with the orb of the yellow-white supergiant filling two of the slant screens like an iconic aureole around the golden-robed angel. The shining arms of the latter are still raised in the gesture of blessing by which he'd sent them on their way; the visual effect suggests that they've never left the spot and that the adventurous interval was an illusion. Any prospect of such an illusion, however, is quickly shattered by the angel extending his arms toward them in a gesture of greeting, and again speaking to them audibly over the ship's angelic operating system.

Sadr: The visible exhilaration showing on your faces clearly means that your visitation to my little planet has made an ecstatic impression upon y'all. Therefore I invite you, one at a time and ladies first, to ask any questions you desire about what you have experienced.

Sophia: O blessed being, you who govern so splendid a star and so paradisal a planet, I ask you three questions: First, were you present at the holy Synaxis by the lake, among the angelic participants? Second, is the Great Lake, or the Golden City itself, the source of all water on Sadronia? And third, is the nebulosity with newly-forming stars surrounding your own star somehow related to the formation of the new heavens at the End of Time?

Sadr: Astronomer beloved of the Lord, I was not personally present at the lakeside rite, remaining on station to govern the two celestial bodies entrusted to me. To your second question, it is indeed the city, from the fount beneath the throne, that fills the lake and thus the four great rivers which water the whole vast garden of the Lord. Your third touches upon the very mystery of the mission you have fulfilled, or rather nearly fulfilled, for yes, the region of space in which my star exists is being prepared for a cosmic role in the geocentric End of Time. The new stars that are forming, along with certain things y'all witnessed on Sadronia, can be considered visible signs of the preparation that is underway. How about you, Maria?

Maria: O shining intellect, master of the intricate spacetime geometry involved in the management of your star, I also have three questions, or maybe four, as two of them blend together, at least in my mind. First, was the City we saw fully cubic, as in St. John, since we could only see the breadth and height? Second, what is the meaning of the multitudes of white horses we saw, and some of them being apparently drilled in maneuvers by angels? Third, and I guess forth, though I cannot separate the two in my mind, did the Lord really counsel us to marry and have children, and what is the meaning of the encirclement of roses whose fragrance engulfed us as we thought of those marriages?

Sadr: Immaculate mathematician, affirmative to your geometrical question: the glorious city is foursquare in all three spatial dimensions, thus cubic in form. To your equestrian query, these are the steeds to be ridden by the hosts of the Lord when He comes to Earth at the End of its Time, and the spirits you saw training them are among those who will ride in that apocalyptic raid. Now to the questions your heart has blended into one, I can confirm that our Lord desires for you to marry as paired, after your return to Earth, and for each couple to bear at least one child. Finally, our Lord wished you to land in the Rose Court, as He calls it, partly because of the very counsel He would give you, and partly for the symbolism of Paradise, as your poet Dante famously sang of it, and as your theologian Luther included it in his seal. But now let us see what is on Maxim's mind.

Maxim: O angelic priest, you who've assisted our Lord in this awesome liturgy, I too come before you with three questions: To begin with, our experience on Sadronia essentially took the place of the purely visionary experiences provided by the other four stars. Does this mean our experience here was also essentially visionary? Also, what is the meaning of the presence of Enoch and Elijah? And finally, what in the world happened when our Lord rinsed the ciborium in the Lake?

Sadr: Adeptest of deacons, and faithful priest to be, your experience on Sadronia was truly visionary, indeed prophetic, in the fullest sense of the words. Yet there remains a real distinction between the duration y'all enjoyed there, from the Rose Court to the Great Lake and back again, and the visionary forms you beheld on your screens during the preceding journey. On Sadronia y'all were incorporated into the vision, which itself is embodied in the very substance of the planet, a substance more subtle than that of Earth. Enoch and Elijah, since each was taken up alive by the Lord, have dwelt quietly on Sadronia, awaiting the moment that will take them back to Earth in order to testify against Antichrist. Since y'all are destined to live until that moment, and may have occasion to encounter them on Earth, it is fitting that you should meet and commune with them here. Lastly, when our Lord rinsed into the Lake the residue of His eucharistic body and blood, brought from the planet where He became incarnate, this consecrated symbol of the new creation, right from the hand of its Firstborn, precipitated an eschatological transmutation of the water, which ultimately irrigates the whole continental garden, and caused the city to arise out of the lake. But I can see Christopher is fairly bursting with questions.

Christopher: O celestial spirit, you who know these distinctions of substance by nature, I would indeed learn more of the ontological state in which we subsisted on Sadronia, which you say was a vision embodied in the planetary substance, a substance more subtle than Earth's. We actually experienced it as being much like the aeviternal ambience we enjoy here in the ship. Then too, the eschatological transmutation caused by the Lord's action presumably introduces another ontological distinction between the planet's natural substance, already more subtle than Earth's, and its transmuted substance. Please expand a bit on these distinctions. Then, I recall being briefed by my astronomer and bride-to-be that your star, like Deneb, is moving directly toward Earth. Is this motion in any way related to the preparation of the new heavens, transpiring in your celestial region? Lastly, what is the ciborium's function in the Participator, and what is the significance of the Lord's refilling it with lake water?

Sadr: Marvelous metaphysician, you have astutely surmised the two key distinctions of substance involved in your experience of Sadronia, first between the natural substance of the planet and that of Earth, and then between the former substance and its transmuted mode. Thus two distinctions and three modes of substance: Earthan, Sadronian natural, and Sadronian transmuted. The natural substance of Sadronia is more subtle than Earth's in the sense that its ambience is essentially aeviternal, which is why you experienced such continuity on emerging from the vessel. The transmutation of the planetary waters and the emergence of the city from the lake signal the beginning of the transmutation of the whole substance of the planet into the eschatological mode of subsistence. On the Day at the End of geocentric Time, my system and that of the companion you mention will undergo extreme and sudden acceleration toward Earth by a catastrophic contraction of spacetime, bringing my region into contact with Earth's unregenerate domain and precipitating the dissolution of the chemical elements of matter with subnuclear fire. Then, as the dead rise along with those who live to the End, the horses you beheld will see action, and the City you saw rising you will see descending. As for the golden ciborium, the sacramental presence of the Lord serves as the focus of angelic devotion that powers your starship. Since the eschatological transmutation rendered the water of the lake ontologically equivalent to the eucharistic host, it serves the purpose, as you see.

As the angel pauses in his discourse, the attention of our Metaphysicals is drawn to the screens showing the orb of Sadronia, where a burst of golden radiance is visible in the Great Lake, spreading down the great rivers and their arterial branches and creeks and runs, casting a golden aura over the whole garden continent, and on over the vast Sadronian sea. The four hyperventilate breathlessly in the angelic ambience, taking in the spectacle of the planet's eschatological transmutation, until the angel resumes his discourse.

Sadr: As y'all can see, the moment of Sadronia's transmutation is at hand, and since you are to arrive on Earth simultaneously with the light leaving my star at this moment, it is meet, right, and salutary that y'all promptly depart. Thanks for accepting our hospitality, and see y'all at the End of Time. *Go in Peace! Serve the Lord!*

At this the stalwart captain, although somewhat startled at the suddenness of the instruction, immediately confirms that the Earthbound transposition vector is logged in, activates command mode of the starship *Synaxis*, and issues the specified command:

"*Synaxis*: New Bethlehem, Pennsylvania."

CHAPTER SIX:
A TALE OF TWO WEDDINGS

I.

The reader will recall that, in the headlong rush of our narrative, we left the Reverend Doctor Killgower and the Elder Lavrenty standing in the makeshift starport in New Bethlehem, just as the good ship *Synaxis* disappeared into deep space, and Lavrenty asked Killgower whether he'd seen the angels. The latter admitted he had not, but while nearly overwhelmed with amazement that the miraculous launch had actually transpired, he suggested they step outside and have a look at the sky. He was curious whether the pulsations of the light of the stars of Cygnus, which they had observed in their prophetic dream, would appear in actuality. Besides, the kids would be back in ten minutes, Earth time, and he could use some fresh air.

The stars of the Swan were just becoming visible in the dimming light of dusk, if you knew where to look, and the two men watched there intently for over five minutes, when the Elder indicated that he wished to keep watch over the landing site while the Reverend Doctor continued to scrutinize the stars. This the latter was happy to do, but as his watch ticked closer to 7:10, the slated time of return, he moved closer to the door, left open by Lavrenty, casting a quick glance into the still-empty bay where the tall Russian strode in silence. As the mission-synchronized watch indicated the exact moment, both men simultaneously exclaimed with joy, the Dean because the five stars had all pulsated at once, and the Elder because the cerulean starship had reappeared promptly in its bay.

The two old men solemnly faced the ship's hatch, as the captain removed the inner seal and then the outer, upon which he stooped and emerged from the vessel, stepping spritely onto terra firma after what seemed like exceedingly more then ten minutes! The two young ladies quickly followed, with Maxim bringing up the rear, and joyous embraces all around quickly ensued. Both elders noticed at once, and remarked approvingly, on the state of high animation and exuberant spirit in which the four young folk had emerged from their plunge into outer space. The young ladies were virtually blushing with ebullience, and their young men, though more restrainedly, were also radiant with joy.

As the voyagers breathed deeply of the air of Earth, tinged with an antique hint of peanut butter, they quickly realized how ravenously hungry they felt. This contingency had been anticipated by Mama Eckhart, who had sent along a basket of healthy snacks, including apples and other fruit, to hold them over until they got back to the farm for a late supper. First, though, they changed out of their vestments and back into their house clothes, leaving the albs and cinctures folded neatly on their respective seats in the quiescent starship. Then, after assuring the site was in order and secured, they piled into Dean Killgower's van and headed north, the Metaphysicals tucking into the picnic basket while uttering sententious fragments of a narrative that would eventually describe the remarkable voyage they had just concluded.

The Dean had to slow once for a couple of deer crossing a wooded stretch of road, but soon they were turning into the farm lane, past a field of ripened corn on their right, and pulling up to the big white farmhouse. To say that they were greeted warmly by the Elder Eckharts would be an understatement, and to their great surprise the Lossky-Mendes elders, Sergei and Manuela, were also on the front porch to greet them, having flown up that day to welcome them back. Considering the sheer number of hugs that were exchanged between the ten people on the porch, and then a renewed round of the same when Sophie and Maria, almost simultaneously, blurted out, "we're getting married!", it was some time before things had settled sufficiently for the group to gather at table.

Seated next to Thomas Killgower was Sergei Lossky, the obvious progenitor of his handsome son, tall and broad-shouldered but spare in figure, his hair and beard greying, a professor of literature specializing in Dostoevsky and

Solzhenitsyn. At his side sat his wife Manuela, a scion of Mexican-American sheep and goat ranchers, whose eye and smile could be seen in the face of her daughter. An accomplished watercolorist and icon writer, Manuela was also an avid reader of classic literature. Across from her sat Rosa Eckhart, whose facial likeness was detectable and whose light brown color was undeniable in both of her children. A devoted farm wife whose accomplishments in that vocation were substantial, several of Rosa's creative talents were much exercised in the Church. By her side, across from Sergei Lossky, was John Eckhart, whose blue eyes and sandy hair could be seen in both twins, and whose stocky build was much like his son's. John had taken a degree in geology before taking over the family farm, and still liked to "play at it", as he was fond of saying. Next to the two fathers their sons were seated, and next to them their sisters, with Killgower and Lavrenty at the heads of the table.

The latter was amply spread for a supper both simple and sufficient, and several large pitchers of beer had appeared, upon the announcement of certain marriages. Conversation was genial and lively, forming mostly around remarks from our four adventurers upon such subjects as the aeviternal ambience which they had inhabited, the astronomical catechism in which they had been instructed, the paradisal planet which they had visited, the preparations for the End of Time that they had witnessed, and the extraordinary manner in which they had been informed they were to marry and bear children. The interest that was generated in these matters could hardly be exhausted in the course of a supper that had started late, on a Monday evening with an early morning ahead.

Sleeping room was found for everyone in the big white farmhouse, and breakfast was served promptly at 7:00 Tuesday morning, with Maria, Sophie, and Manuela assisting Rosa with the pancakes, sausage, and eggs. Conversation quickly resumed where it had subsided the night before, as the strong coffee performed its office, and several things were quickly resolved. Lavrenty and Killgower needed a couple of days to properly debrief the four and to communicate with the Russian hermits and the Evangelical prophets, after which the Lossky-Mendes twins would accompany their parents back to Texas while the young Eckharts stayed in Pennsylvania. The betrothed and their parents would be in close contact with regard to wedding plans, the development of which would fulfill cherished hopes of young and old alike, and the betrothed in particular made it clear that the events were not to be long forestalled. Their plan for the day was for Killgower, Lavrenty, and the four Metaphysicals to spend the morning in Christopher's study discussing the occurrences comprised in the just-completed mission, while John Eckhart turned the hay he'd mown two days earlier, Rosa and Manuela cleaned up from breakfast and prepared the midday meal, and Sergei caught up on some academic communications. In the afternoon, The Reverend Doctor and the Elder would confer by phone with their contacts while Maria and Sophie joined their mothers in the farmhouse, and their fiancés, along with

Sergei Lossky, helped John Eckhart get the third-cutting hay into the barn.

As the six sat down in the loft study, the first thing Killgower wanted to talk about was the curious observation of the five stars of Cygnus pulsating simultaneously, at the same instant *Synaxis* had reappeared. This had perplexed him at first, but on reflection he'd realized that if each of the aeviternal visits of the starship to the five planets had occurred at the moment each star emitted the light that would reach Earth at the same time as their return, then one would expect to see the indicative pulsations of starlight arrive all at once, at the same time as *Synaxis*, just as observed. This analysis was greeted with smiles and acclamations that this, indeed, made perfect sense. Thus launched, the scheduled discussion ensued, guided by penetrating questions from the two old men, with the intention of assembling an orderly account of the mission's outcome to be conveyed to those circles in Russia and in America whose support had been crucial.

The patient reader of the preceding two chapters is already in possession of the substantial content of that account: the tingling intellectuality and breathless hyperventilation of the ambience they had shared with the angels; the graciousness of the angelic beings themselves, and of their catechetical artistry; the nearly-unbelievable beauty of Sadronia, with a night sky like the blue of a clear day on Earth, and a daytime sky of brilliant yellow-white; the gracefulness of the unicorns bearing them between the

Rose Court of the Christ Child and the shore of the Great Lake, where the Child flew in on the back of a giant swan, and from a small stone altar on the shore led a synaxis of angels in the *Sanctus* and distributed His own Body and Blood, consecrated on the planet of His Sacrifice, to the four of them and to Enoch and Elijah. The reader will also remember that the divine Child subsequently rinsed the gold ciborium in the Lake, precipitating a transfiguration of its waters, and an emergence or ascension from these shining waters of a great foursquare City, such as was seen by St. John in his Apocalypse. Then too, the angel of Sadr explained the role his system would play in the End of Time on Earth, brought into collision by a contraction of spacetime—a scenario that included the thousands of white horses they'd seen being trained by angels, on Sadronia.

When the two old men were satisfied they had achieved a good understanding of this account, and once they had prepared detailed notes from which they could communicate its substance to the others, Lavrenty raised again the question of the Adversary and his legions. As expected, the degree of divine protection provided via angelic operators assigned to this mission had prevented any detectable intervention by demonic powers, even though he himself had watched for any trace of evil spirits in the starship's bay. He then asked the others to consider carefully whether they could recall anything suspicious in this regard. After a considerable pause, the Metaphysicals affirmed their agreement with the Elder's assessment, but the Reverend Doctor remained silent, with furrowed brow.

At length he admitted that, while there was nothing tangible to point to, he nevertheless harbored a certain unease on the subject, given the known characteristics of the enemy, and not least his subtlety. In any event, the main thing was to remain vigilant going forward, and speaking of going forward, it occurred to the Reverend Doctor that provision would have to be made to secure the starship, preferably here on the farm. *Synaxis* could remain temporarily in its original bay, on a rental basis, but a more permanent base should be established as soon as feasible. Christopher responded that he thought his father would be amenable to building a hangar on the farm, and most of the lumber could probably be furnished from their woodlands and sawed in their mill, but a bit of financial support for other materials might be needed.

Their morning session ended with the morning itself, as the dinner bell began to chime, and the six made their way to the farmhouse for the noon meal. At table, John Eckhart agreed they would build a hangar for *Synaxis* in late fall, after all the crops were in, if Chris would design it and specify the lumber, which he figured they could saw from the pile of aged logs he'd accumulated for future needs. But speaking of getting in the crops, it was time to get started baling, hauling, pitching and stacking the ten acres of orchard grass and fescue that John Eckhart had turned over in the morning. The two girls did some harvesting from the garden, washing the produce carefully in the kitchen sink while their mothers had a cup of tea before starting supper. The rest of the day passed swiftly; the hay was in, the supper ready, the conversation relaxed and slightly jubilant. Evening dimmed into night, and everyone slept the sleep of the justified—even Lavrenty kept vigil for only two hours.

Wednesday morning dawned clear and bright, and over breakfast it was decided to more or less repeat the previous day's schedule, with the six conferring in the morning to wrap up the mission debriefing in view of responses from Orthodox and Evangelical authorities. As for the afternoon, John Eckhart had been so happy with the extra help getting in the hay that he asked the same crew to help pick, haul, and unload fifteen acres of corn, to which all had heartily agreed.

Christopher's loft study was fragrant with the new hay just outside the door, when the Metaphysicals and the two old men sat down to conclude their immediate considerations regarding the Cygnus mission. The report from Russia was that several hermits had witnessed the simultaneous flash or pulsation of the five principal stars, α- through ε-Cygni, at dusk on the Exaltation of the Holy Cross. They also had sensed something they described as a qualitative change in the atmosphere, affecting them almost like a trance or rapture, in which they had thought distinctly of the starship *Synaxis* and had felt the profound importance of preserving it. The Patriarchate had concurred with their belief that the Lord might have further missions in store. As for Killgower's "invisible college" of Evangelicals, a series of dreams had befallen a number of them during the night of the voyagers' return, which the group had prayerfully pieced together over their network, producing in composite the following: Four stars fell upon the Earth, precipitating a sunrise, then another, until seven suns, each brighter than its predecessor, stood brilliantly above the horizon. Then, one by one, the seven suns set, gradually darkening the Earth to total night. They were still discussing the interpretation of the prophecy, but the idea was gaining ground that the return of the four stars had signaled the beginning of a fourteen-year period terminating with the End of Time. The first seven years would be a final flowering of Restoration, and the final seven would be the biblical term of the Antichrist's ascendance and reign, according to this view.

The Metaphysicals looked at one another, all thinking the same thing: If this interpretation were true, not only would *they* never see forty years of age, but any kids they had would barely have time to become teenagers. Lavrenty looked thoughtful, noting that Moscow was still considering this interpretation. Then *a propos* of the Russian concern with securing the starship, he asked Christopher if he had any thoughts on the "hangar." Indeed the captain was already thinking of a foursquare post-and-beam base, thirty-two feet on a side and sixteen feet high, with a carbon-rod superstructure in the form of a pyramidal rising from the four corners to a peak thirty-two feet above the floor, and covered with silicone-coated fiberglass. The materials and construction labor required for the covered superstructure, plus the concrete for footer and floor, would comprise the major costs that would have to be subsidized. By quick estimate, it appeared that sufficient funds remained in the account Killgower had established to finance the mission; furthermore, assurances were given that supplemental funding would be available to fill any unexpected gaps.

The dinner bell again brought an end to their deliberations, and after a brief rest, the corn was picked and hauled by supper time, with just two wagons still to be unloaded. The Reverend Doctor and the Russian Elder had departed shortly after midday, the former to return to his office at the College, where a new term was underway, after dropping off the latter at the airport, from where he would fly back to Russia. Since the Lossky-Mendes family would be leaving Thursday morning, the four affianced lovers devoted the evening to their respective spouses-to-be (while their parents chatted amiably), in the course of which conversation it was firmly decided that both couples would be wed before year-end. On this happy note the Metaphysicals parted the following morning, bursting with eager plans.

II.

It would be just over three months until our brides-to-be were united with their bridegrooms, the date of December 27, the Feast of St. John, having been quickly settled upon for the weddings of both couples, Chris and Sophia, Max and Maria. It was further decided that they would be married in a single ceremony, to be held in the College Chapel at Luther Aquinas, amid the tall stained glass depicting the

Old and New Testaments and the chief Sacraments. The rite would be Russian Orthodox, with Elder Lavrenty (at his own request) officiating, and by dispensation from the Patriarchate, the Reverend Doctor Killgower assisting.

With these essentials established, the two young ladies devoted much of October to bonding with their mothers in the joy of the coming events—and deciding the details of the reception and their dresses—while also preparing for a two-week seminar thy were to give at Creation A&M in November. The theologian of the group, meanwhile, was in conference with his diocesan superiors regarding the findings of the mission he had been granted leave to pursue, as well as the plans for his ordination toward the end of November. By then Maria and Sophie would be finished with their work in Colorado, and Chris should have the building to house *Synaxis* in pretty good shape. Thus, all three could make it to Texas for his ordination and a quick visit, before the Eckharts flew back to Pennsylvania. Our metaphysical farmer, in turn, had soybeans to pick and more corn, after which he would roast and grind a few months' supply of animal feed, but by mid-October he and father John were ready to saw the lumber for the new "silo."

The two had decided that "silo" was what they would call the new building, which would stand back from the big red barn (as seen from the farmhouse), behind the two equipment sheds and more or less parallel with the mill. A less unusual name than "hangar" or "spaceport," in the context of a farmstead, seemed more prudent from a security perspective. The exact whereabouts of this marvelous vessel, after all, might best be kept secret. Chris had been able to rough out a design and draw up a list of the lumber required, making use of a stack of sixteen-foot logs harvested from the woodlands over several years. Sawing from this timber, they would need sixteen 6"x 6" posts, sixteen 2"x 6" planks for the top and bottom plates, and twenty-four 1" x 6" boards for lathing between the posts. The pyramidal gridwork of the roof structure would consist of carbon-fiber rods produced by the same vendor he'd used for the *Synaxis* project, as likewise the silicone-glass sheeting. The silo would be assembled by a crew from the manufacturer in New Bethlehem. By early November the concrete pad was poured, and the lumber was ready for the raising.

His sister and his fiancee, meanwhile, were off to Colorado to present some of the new geometry and astronomy they had they had learned as a result of their collaboration with angelic intelligences. Maria's presentations were mainly concerned with the actual hypergeometric navigation of the voyage, along with what she had learned about the interactions of angelic intelligence with the physical geometry of spacetime. For Sophia's part, the two astronomical discoveries she chose to highlight were the explanation of the "double spectrum" of Gienah as an intentional duplication by its governing angel, and the existence of the amazing planet Sadronia, a number of whose features she described in detail without going into the remarkable adventure they'd had there. She also had some things to say about linguistic aspects of their angelic encounters, the communication of meaning in articulated starlight, and the audible verbalization and musical expressions they'd experienced. Their seminars were received with some interest, and after two weeks of lecturing, answering questions, and generally conversing on their chosen topics and related matters, the two were happy to escape to Texas, where Maria's beloved was waiting and where Sophie's would soon be joining them.

Maxim, in the meantime, had been back in the saddle, riding the Lucky M between ecclesiastical meetings until the date of his ordination arrived, at which time he would be installed in the parish he would be serving. The latter, as it turned out, was located on the outskirts of San Angelo, a thriving city of about 120,000, on the Concho River roughly sixty miles north of the family ranch. Max's parents were naturally delighted with the distance, given the large territory covered by the diocese, and were happily present in the small Orthodox church on the appointed day, accompanied by the three other Metaphysicals including his betrothed. In most cases a young priest, provided he was not taking monastic vows, was expected to be married before his ordination, but since the wedding was now barely a month away, and since the congregation needed him, it had been decided to proceed. The actual rite would be carried out during Divine Liturgy, in this case the Western Rite of St. Gregory, since this congregation had been established as a mission to ex-Roman Catholics disillusioned with the Roman hierarchy.

St. Michael and All Angels Russian Orthodox Church had been modeled on the old adobe missions which are proliferous in the American Southwest, but with typical Eastern features: a cross atop the westward-facing entrance, aligned with another cross surmounting the dome of the nave. Adornment of the interior with holy icons was still underway, as funds became available, but already Christ Pantokrator looked down from inside the dome, Theotokos and Christ Child graced the eastern wall behind the altar, and St. Michael with other angels covered the iconostasis. The rubrical propers and ordinaries of the Mass were solemnly chanted by priests, choir, and congregation in ancient harmonic modes, filling the nave with a resonant ambience that somewhat reminded our Metaphysicals of their experience in the *aeviternum*. It was indeed as though the angels themselves were present as an older priest, Maxim's mentor from Seminary, led the young candidate forward among the angelic ranks adorning the iconostasis, to the altar. Kneeling, Maxim rested his head against the altar. The bishop then, rising from his seat, placed his stole and his right hand on Maxim's head, solemnly intoning the prayers, declarations, and admonishments of the Sacrament of Ordination. The Divine Liturgy concluded with Holy Communion and the Prayer, Dismissal, and Blessing that followed, before the final reading, John 1: 1-14, which ended, "And the Word became flesh, and dwelt among us, and we beheld His glory, the glory as of the only-begotten of the Father, full of grace and truth." With that, a smiling Father Maxim Lossky-Mendes was ready to receive the joyful congratulations of family, friends, and fiancée.

Chris and Maria flew back to Pennsylvania two days later, after Maria had inspected the parsonage where she and Max would be living, and had herself been rather closely inspected by members of the congregation, whose *matrushka* she was to become. Besides, the Eckhart twins felt real affection for their inlaws-to-be, Sergei and Manuela, and were happy to spend a couple of days visiting with them, not to mention that they wouldn't see their betrothed again for almost a month. Back at the farm, Christopher found that the carbon-rod roofing frame of the new silo had nearly been completed by the crew in his absence, as well as the wrapping of the foursquare base with silicone-glass. Chris had decided to cover the base with the same high-performance sheeting as the roof, slit to 54" width for overlapping on the lathwork so that four courses of the sheeting would cover the base, and also fit the transverse supports in the triangular faces of the pyramid roof. The silicone elastomer forming the outer surface of the sheeting was dyed a deep red for the base, with metallic grey for the roofing, so the new silo would blend right in with the barn and other outbuildings.

By early December the building was completed to the captain's satisfaction, including a simple wooden structure in the center of the floor, in which the polyhedral outer shell of *Synaxis* would nestle stably. The ship's geometer had assisted in designing this, and Maria had also worked out the details of the translation vector by which the spacecraft would be moved from the bay in New Bethlehem to its new home on the farm. Since as far as they knew, all four of the crew had to be on the ship for the activation rite, the plan was to move the ship while the Texans were there for the wedding. And since the Lossky-Mendes family would be arriving on the 23rd to spend Christmas, Christopher proposed that they move the ship on Christmas Eve, the date of both of the visions in which the Child had given him the design.

Accordingly, this is exactly what they did. After late Mass at the Eckharts' church, their parents dropped off the four at the old factory, where they found *Synaxis* safe and sound, and their vestments folded on the seats where they'd left them. Since it was cold, they donned the albs over their other clothing. After laying aside their winter coats, they tied the sky-blue cinctures around their waists, and assumed their stations for the activation rite. The newly-ordained chaplain reminded the crew of the simple fourfold sequence, then led them reverently through it, concluding with the doxology, "Praise Father, Son, and Holy Ghost." As they sang the "Amen," the familiar scintillations and tinglings of the angelic ambience filled the interior of the vessel, prompting the captain to proceed by invoking "command mode". The destination term for the translation vector Maria had constructed for the move was simply "Home", since the new silo on the Eckhart farm was to be the starship's "home base." At the command, "*Synaxis*: Home," therefore, the cerulean spheroid disappeared from the manufacturing bay in which it had been assembled, and simultaneously appeared in the silo which had been prepared for it, resting solidly in its new wooden nest.

Leaving their vestments on board as before, the happy lovers walked through the cold starlit darkness, over frozen ground illuminated by a thin dusting of snow, past the outbuildings and the barn to the farmhouse with its candle-lit windows. As they walked, Max and Maria, Chris and Sophia hand in hand, it seemed to them that the ambience of the angels accompanied them, as though their angelic crew, having just conveyed *Synaxis* to the farm, were hanging around to celebrate the Nativity with them. Although it was already late, no plans were made to rise early on Christmas Day. Breakfast was set for 10:00 and the feeding of the animals deferred accordingly. Thus the two families sat up surprisingly late—they didn't know where the time had gone—and the angels, as it were, sat up with them. That is, not only were Chris and Sophia, Max and Maria aware of the angelically altered ambience, from previous experience, but John and Rosa, Sergei and Manuela, who had never before encountered this quality of breathless hyperventilation, also decidedly noticed its supersensory scintillations. Indeed, as the Metaphysicals realized later, the presence of the angels explained "where the time had gone".

Christmas Day 2041 was glorious. The sky shone clear and bright, and the dusting of snow lent an aspect of brilliance to the farmstead and fields. Everyone had enjoyed a good night's sleep, and after Father Maxim led Morning Prayer, a marvelous breakfast was served, over which remembrances of their exhilarating Christmas Eve mingled with anticipations of the events to follow in just two days. As for the former, the elders affirmed there had been "something in the air," and their offspring assured them that the "something" had been angelic; while the latter included both immediate matters pertaining to the next two days, and general plans for after the wedding. For the rest of Christmas Day and the day after (the Feast of Stephen), the betrothed were free to romance one another, walking or riding the farm and surrounding roads, having a quiet lunch in New Bethlehem while their parents dined at the farm, etc. In the late afternoon of St. Stephen's, both families would drive to the College, where Dean Killgower had reserved the guest house for the brides-to-be and their parents, and a dormitory suite for the two bridegrooms. Since the Feast of St. John was a Sunday, they would be married after a 10:00 Divine Liturgy (according to the Rite of St. Tikhon), the wedding to be followed by a luncheon reception and celebration in the College gymnasium. As for their honeymoon, to no one's surprise they were going together to a quiet little lodge on Lake Erie, where separate quarters awaited them for the long-desired consummation of their nuptial vows.

After the honeymoon Max and Maria would fly back to Texas, where St. Michael and All Angels awaited them, parsonage included. Chris and Sophia would move into a suite of rooms in the big white farmhouse to begin with, until Chris could build a separate house on the farm. Such were the topics of conversation over breakfast on that bright Christmas Day, and such was the joy that animated their talk, that again an analogy of angelic presence supervened, as though their invisible visitors of the evening before were still with them. Furthermore, all were delighted to find that the impression of this presence persisted all of Christmas Day—even feeding the animals was an entirely new experience—and throughout the Feast of Stephen as well, so that they happily found themselves checking into their quarters at the College, on the eve of the wedding, wondering how in the world the time the time had passed so quickly.

III.

December 27, 2043, was a halcyon day in the heart of winter, the temperature having risen into the low 30s overnight so that the first hour after sunrise sufficed to melt the thin crust of snow, and by the time everyone arrived for Divine Liturgy (and its sequel) the still-green lawns of the College glistened with snowmelt. Inside the chapel, sunlight streamed aslant through the Old Testament glass on the south wall, colored light from the Wisdom window falling on the Lossky-Mendes family where they stood, across the center aisle from the Eckharts, whose location on the north side of the nave was under the Gospels window. The dark wood of the high-arched ceiling contrasted beautifully with the polychrome brilliance of the tall windows. Even the New Testament glass on the north side received enough indirect sunlight to show its colors. Four large icons graced the chancel railing—Christ Pantokrator, Theotokos and Christ Child, St. John the Theologian, and

Synaxis of Angels—and the choir chanted psalmody while the assembly gathered.

Elder Lavrenty, in full Orthodox priestly garb, and Reverend Doctor Killgower in alb, surplice and stole, solemnly led the congregation through the Western Rite based on an Anglican order, which St. Tikhon had composed, and of which the reader has had a small taste in chapter three. At the completion of the Liturgy, as the closing Gospel was being chanted, the brides and their grooms withdrew to the rear of the church. There each was handed a lighted candle as Lavrenty chanted from the front, "Let us pray to the Lord," to which the congregation responded, "Lord, have mercy." As this exchange was repeated twice more, the couples advanced very slowly toward the front, holding the candles in their right hands. "Blessed are all they that fear the Lord," the Elder continued, and as they reached the front he made the sign of the cross over them, chanting, "Blessed is the kingdom of the Father and of the Son and of the Holy Ghost."

Next, each of the four was presented with a beautiful purple and gold crown, which they first reverently kissed and with which they were then solemnly crowned. Killgower chanted St. Paul's admonitions to husbands and wives, his deep baritone resounding in the high nave, then Lavrenty intoned the Gospel of Jesus turning water into wine at a wedding feast in Cana of Galilee, concluding with the Lord's Prayer. Maxim and Maria, Christopher and Sophia, were then asked, one by one, if they had promised themselves to anyone other than their betrothed, and whether they would take their betrothed as husband or wife. Their easily audible denials to the first question, and affirmations to the second, led to the pronouncement that then and thenceforth Maxim and Maria were one flesh, Christopher and Sophia were one flesh. To seal their unions, each received a sip of wine from a golden cup proffered by the Elder.

Now Lavrenty made the sign of the cross over Maxim and Maria, kissed their right hands and joined them together, covering their joined hands with his stole, while Killgower did the same with Christopher and Sophia. To the accompaniment of joyous singing, the two old men slowly led the couples in procession around the nave, returning to the front where, standing before the holy icons, they offered admonitions and counsel to the smiling newlyweds. With this final solemnity completed, the congregation began singing, "God grant them many years, God grant them many years, God grant them many years…," as the ecstatic couples slowly recessed to the rear, the new husbands carrying small icons of Christ, and their wives of the Virgin Theotokos.

And so it was that our Metaphysicals were wed, although the foregoing narrative barely hints at the splendor of their wedding, framed by the tall and glorious glass of the Old and New Testaments, and the Sacramental windows at the front, with the rich and moving modes of Orthodox hymnody resounding in the high nave. The reception was splendidly catered by the College food service, the fare simple but plenteous, and the atmosphere that permeated the gymnasium, absorbing the ceremonious toasts and roasts, the music and the dancing, was not only predictably charged with delight and hilarity. For those in the know something else was present, something supersensory tinged with intellect. That presence reigned over the happy celebration on that bright, halcyon winter's day, something that brought with it a quality of timelessness.

In no time at all, therefore, they found that the hugs and kisses and farewells (though doubtless not the angels) were behind them, and they were climbing into Chris's station wagon, their luggage stowed in back, and pulling out of the College en route to that quiet little lodge on Lake Erie. Sophie rode "shotgun" beside Chris, and Max and Maria sat behind them, as they drove blissfully through the winter woods toward their destination, the car's interior filled with genial chatter. We shall not pursue our Metaphysicals into the long-awaited intimacies of their bridal chambers, but rather, we modestly bring the present romance to its close.

EPILOGUE:
THE REUNION DISCOURSE

"On behalf of Luther-Aquinas Evangelical College, it is my privilege to welcome our class of 2040, on the occasion of your five-year reunion, to this reception in honor of four of your classmates. A number of you were here five years ago for their Valedictory Symposium, and are no doubt curious about any changes of intellectual perspective that may have occurred in the course of their remarkable adventure, and the quiet notoriety it has caused."

The Reverend Doctor Killgower, in his role as Dean of the College, addressed a sizeable gathering of alumnae and other interested parties in the Ox & Swan tavern, on an early evening in late May 2045. Tables had been pushed to the side and extra chairs set up for the occasion, facing the table at the end of the room, under the massive painting of the Dominican Ox and the Augustinian Swan, where our Metaphysicals were seated. But behold, they were no longer only four: on Christopher's knee sat a bouncing baby boy, somewhat more than a year old, and on Maxim's a bright-eyed little girl of about the same age. Handing the child to her beaming mother, Maxim rose to speak, first thanking everyone for their interest in what he and the other three had discovered, and then noting that, as the theologian in their midst, he would focus his remarks on a point of prophecy.

"We will be happy to answer any questions on the mission we undertook, and to discuss any related issues that arise. But what I want to call to your attention is a prophecy received through a series of dreams by certain Evangelical sages, and the interpretation which has been affirmed by the Orthodox hierarchy. The composite vision is this: After four stars fall to the Earth, seven suns arise, one after the other, making everything brighter and brighter. Then, one at a time, the suns set, making everything darker and darker. The interpretation is this: The return of us four from Cygnus initiated a sequence of fourteen years, of which the first seven represent a final flowering of our Eliatic Restoration, and the second seven represent the ascendancy of Antichrist. What I have just described, in other words, is a "final fortnight of years" culminating sometime in 2057 (for we know not the day nor the hour, nor even the month), and of which we are already in year number two. Believe it or not, for this is not an article of faith; however, this is the prophetic data I commend to your solemn consideration."

After taking a few questions on this startling announcement, in the course of which the other Metaphysicals chimed in on particular points, Maxim returned to his seat (and his glass of imperial stout), smiling at Maria dandling their little girl on her lap. Now it was Christopher's turn to hand off the little tyke he'd been holding to Sophia, who delightedly snuggled him in her lap, whispering softly into his ear. Rising to his feet, the stocky metaphysician restated his predecessor's thanks to the friends and classmates assembled to honor, not them, but the Lord who had gifted and empowered them for achievement.

"It is a solemn consideration indeed, that less then thirteen years may remain until the End of Time. Equally solemn, to anyone who takes this possibility seriously, is the question of how best to fill those years to the glory of God. As for me and my house, we shall focus on the biblical sciences of nature which, while following the scientific method in judging theories by comparing them with facts and data of nature, nevertheless derive the general shapes of the theories to be thus judged from the data of Scripture. From creation cosmology through flood geology and creation biology to biblical anthropology and linguistics, we stand today at the culmination of nearly a century of hard and brilliant work by biblical scientists, which is ripe for a synthesis. As a metaphysician and philosopher of science, I shall concentrate on the metaphysical foundations of these sciences, especially the relations of their theoretical structures to the written Word of God, and thereby to His eternal Word. As a husband and father, meanwhile, I shall stand by my wife and my son through bright years and dark, in the mercy of our Lord Jesus Christ."

As Christopher sat down, before he could even reach for his glass of Augustiner, his little boy reached for him, emphatically enough that Sophie simply handed him back to his dad. Since the little girl was still settled on Maria's lap, our brown-eyed brunette rose to add her remarks to those of her husband and her brother. Sophia began with a quick review of the major astronomical findings of their mission into outer space, including the corresponding angelology and linguistics, and then continued.

"I am pleased to join my husband, as well as my father-in-law, the flood geologist, in the project just commended to your pursuit and support. A coherent set of theoretical models formed from biblical data, then suitably mathematized in order to explain the natural data better than competing secular models—that is what we are after! As an astronomer I shall work with my sister-in-law, although at a distance this time, on geometrical aspects of large-scale cosmological structure as well as star formation, while consulting closely with my husband on the metaphysics, especially regarding the role of formal causation. As a linguist I am especially interested in biblical models of the origin and dispersion of human language groups, deriving from the Babel narrative in Genesis. Given that, by way of the stars, we have direct access to angelic intelligence, I have hopes of assistance from that quarter as well. As a wife and mother, I am grateful for the gift of marriage to this man, and for the chance to bring up this child in our Lord Jesus Christ, who asked that we conceive and bear him, for whatever years there may be."

At this point Sophia's voice thickened somewhat with emotion, whereupon with a formal smile and a quick nod she took her seat. Meanwhile the little girl, who like her cousin was beginning to show signs of restlessness, had been handed back to her daddy, freeing Maria to rise and speak in turn, her blue eyes characteristically atwinkle. She began by thanking her sister-in-law for the offer of further collaboration, and offered her enthusiastic support for her brother's challenging project—a crowning synthesis of the biblical creation sciences.

"With regard to cosmology, we shall need to settle the question of the validity of Einstein's relativistic equations in 4-dimensional spacetime, for the Humphreysian type of geocentric white hole models depend on these equations. Should the Einsteinian formalism prove to be invalid, we shall need another way of explaining the "young Earth/ancient stars" paradox, possibly involving a formal causality operating from the *aeviternum* and expressing as physical spacetime. A more adequate theory might be developed along the lines of what I learned from the angels, about how they control the physical geometrics of their stars by direct intellectual operation, only generalized to encompass the whole universe. Of course, that's only one possibility. But anyway, if we look to the prophecy, we have five-and-a-half brightening years plus however many of the others, to see what the Lord will allow us, and empower us, to accomplish. Most important of all, however, because all the intellectual work presupposes them, are the dear obligations I have vowed to my marvelous husband, and the promises I made when we baptized our baby boy, for these are the foundations of my life in Christ."

Just then, as if they had somehow conspired, both of the little ones let out shrieks of impatience, and began squirming to get down and run, to the great amusement of the assembled classmates of 2040 and the other interested parties. The Dean, who was ceremoniously attired in his tartan jacket for the occasion, promptly suggested adjournment to the courtyard outside, where the kids could tire themselves out while those who still had questions for our Metaphysicals could further converse with them. This proposal played out beautifully, as the little boy and girl just arrived at the awareness of being undeniably tired at about the same time their parents' interlocutors were winding down as well. It was already dark as the two young families strolled slowly, almost leisurely, under the campus lights to the lot where the Eckhart SUV was parked. Max and Maria, Chris and Sophia, sauntered hand in hand, with each father carrying his child in the other arm.

Biographical Sketch of the Author

By Jim Henderson, Ph.D.

I first met Larry Rinehart in college. He was a senior major-
ing in Chemistry, soon to graduate *summa cum laude* and be
inducted into Phi Beta Kappa. I was a freshman, captivated
by popular music and beginning the first of three degrees
I went on to earn in religious studies. Larry and I have
remained friends, and sometimes collaborators, for five
decades. Understandably, passing years wrought changes
in our lives. Our religious, political and educational views
developed, and now they often diverge. Nevertheless, the
remarkable intellectual and artistic qualities I respected in
the young Larry have grown only more admirable with
the passage of time. His perseverance in pursuit of good-
ness, truth and beauty; his devotion to contemplation and
independent thinking; his reverence for the earth, its fruits
and creatures; his imaginative vigor and intellectual rigor—
all these aspects of Larry's character inspire, more than ever,
as his writing and faith have matured.

Part of what characterizes Larry is his rootedness in rural
life. He grew up on a 37-acre tract of pasture, gardens,
and woodland in York County, Pennsylvania. There he still
lives, with his wife Donna, surrounded by extended family
and the vegetables, orchard grass, chickens and rabbits

they raise organically and sustainably—sharing any surplus production with the local food pantry. As a young man, Larry was an accomplished wrestler, an earnest Lutheran, an exceptionally bright student, and a rambler with a fondness for the outdoors. Now in his seventy-fifth year, he remains fit, witty and committed to productive, time-proven patterns of husbandry, study, worship and writing.

In the 1970s, after leaving Princeton Theological Seminary to pursue independent studies, Larry earned a livelihood topping trees for Asplundh in Pennsylvania, then harvesting vegetables at the Esalen Institute in California. Later, with a growing family to support, he worked for thirty years as an applied chemist; his technical and administrative responsibilities addressing quality control, research and development at a textile converting plant not far from his home. Retirement in 2009 freed Larry to invest even more time in the spiritual, intellectual and artistic pursuits that shape and sustain his character.

Larry has practiced the craft of writing for upwards of fifty years. His body of work is extensive and carefully articulated, yet not well known. Creating matters more to Larry than marketing. Indeed, self-promotion is anathema to him. However, as a younger adult, Larry was an epic poet, in search of a name for the ages. He immersed himself in the worlds of Homer, Vergil, *Le Chanson de Roland* and *El Cid*, Dante, Milton, Ariosto, and Torquato Tasso's *Gerusalemme Liberata* (1581). Beginning in the later 1970s and continuing into the new millennium,

Larry completed *America Liberata*, an epic poem in 28,561 long verses. Placed on the scales of literary history, this epic of the bard Raginhart (the pseudonym Larry applied to his ambitious "Aquarian" project) contains more lines, words and syllables than do Dante's *Divine Comedy* and Milton's *Paradise Lost* combined. Furthermore, the encyclopedic scope of Larry's epic resembles the classics that inspired it. Its heroic purpose was to comprehend the wisdom of the world's diverse cultural and spiritual traditions, especially as expressed in peaks of the American literary landscape— particularly those shaping the broad tradition of American Romanticism and transcendentalism.

In addition to steadily crafting an epic poem (whose world view and heroic inspiration Larry now repudiates, though he does assert that it ably represents a decadent epoch and accurately symbolizes its misguided values), Larry further developed and exercised his literary voice by writing fiction, works of drama and devotion, lyric poetry (some illustrated by the author himself), instructional material for teaching science, and numerous essays in theology, philosophy, history, and literary and cultural criticism. From 2015-2017 Larry published four volumes of theological and metaphysical writings: *Esse & Evangel, The Knowledge of Christ, Poet of Heaven and Earth, and A Metaphysical Luther*. These books establish an intellectual foundation for the works of high mimetic romantic fiction (see Northrop Frye) that animate his current literary activity. The first of these "romances" to be published is *Outer Space at the End of Time*. Other volumes are in development. However, as

Larry recently told me, "[M]y pen belongs to the Lord. We shall have to see what ensues."

Larry's authorship reflects a decided religious orientation. To encounter Larry Rinehart today, either in person or in print, is to meet an "Evangelical Catholic Orthodox Lutheran"—a Christian whose faith rests in "the Holy Trinity revealed in the Old and New Testaments, and in Jesus Christ to whom these Scriptures testify." In physical appearance, Larry resembles the Amish farmers of neighboring Lancaster County. Certain elements of his personal experience help to illuminate the tone of polemical contentiousness one finds in his non-fiction writings. As a wrestler Larry sought, and often prevailed in, competition. As an advocate of the theory of Intelligent Design, Larry entered public debates via letters to the press regarding the controversial 2005 *Kitzmiller v Dover Area School District* decision in his hometown. As a politically conservative small-scale farmer, Larry's world view shares some common ground with the Christian apocalyptic movement mediated by the best-selling Christian science fiction author Mark Goodwin. Like Mark, Larry argues that contemporary America, and much of Christianity, have both strayed from its principles. His personal calling is to indicate, perhaps with a prophetic tone, a truer path.

Larry acknowledges no earthly master as he lives out this calling, in accord with Matthew 23:10: *Neither be called masters, for you have one master, the Christ*. He is an "individual" in Kierkegaard's sense of the word. As a person of faith, Larry pursues his intellectual work "as a sort of devotion to Christ, intending the furtherance of His name rather than mine." He may strike some of his contemporaries as a medieval mystic transported to the twenty-first century. But make no mistake: Larry is a formidable scholar of ancient and modern Christian tradition, including its Eastern Orthodox, Roman Catholic, and Lutheran strands.

Through decades of independent scholarship Larry acquired the requisite logical, rhetorical, philological, philosophical, and theological training to stand his ground among biblical interpreters, church historians, and religious academicians of all stripes. His hard-won personal perspective (which, he would argue, endeavors to remain true to the Biblical revelation) navigates a specific channel in the history of ideas, one known—through the work of René Guénon, Frithjof Schuon, and Ananda Coomaraswamy—as the *philosophia perennis*. An important corollary Larry derives from this metaphysical stance is "the necessity of attachment to an orthodox spiritual tradition." Embracing that truth, Larry was prompted (c. 2008) "to reclaim my Baptism as a Christian and identity as a Lutheran by resuming regular Word and Sacrament worship … along with daily prayer." "The *philosophia*," Larry declares, "became the crook by which the Shepherd snatched me from the maelstrom."

In addition to the life experiences, intellectual skills, and religious perspectives sketched above, Larry brings to his writing a rare capacity to analyze, interpret and employ the intricacies of earth and space science. He also possesses an even rarer capacity: the ability to critique the assumptions that underlie modern science, its associated methods, and the disciplines those methods define—from geology through materials science to cosmology. One of the rewards of reading *Outer Space at the End of Time* is grappling with the mathematical and scientific concepts its characters must master and apply as they pursue their epic purpose and claim the boons that endeavor secures—as I hope the reader will agree.

Jim Henderson is an educator, musician, composer, writer, and editor. He earned degrees from Gettysburg College (A.B., Religion; summa cum laude, *Phi Beta Kappa, student commencement speaker), Columbia University (M.A., Comparative Study of Religions), and Duke University (Ph.D., Religion and Culture). A member of the Religious Society of Friends (Quakers), Jim worked from 1981-2014 as a teacher and administrator at Carolina Friends School, Durham, NC. Since his teenage years, he has maintained an active professional life as a saxophonist, keyboard player, and song writer/arranger. Jim's* Still Souled Out *recording (2018) is available on Amazon and CD Baby. He is also the creator (2005-2016) of* Ariel's Way, *a modern musical adaptation of William Shakespeare's* The Tempest. *Assisting his wife of forty years, Jan Tedder, Jim has helped to develop* HUG Your Baby, *an international educational program for parents and birth professionals that teaches child development to enhance parenting and breastfeeding success. Jim and Jan are the parents of two adult sons. They (and their partners and a grandchild) all also reside in Durham, North Carolina.*